Siege

Donland and The Hornet

By
Perry Comer

ISBN: 9781075456855

DEDICATION

Chief Petty Officer Phillip Comer

United States Coast Guard

BOOKS BY PERRY COMER

The Prize
(Donland)

The Messenger
Donland and the Hornet

Donland's Ransom
Donland and the Hornet

Raid on Port Royal
Donland and the Hornet

The Bond of Duty
Donland and the Hornet

Siege
Donland and The Hornet

The Snake Killer
(Juvenile Action/adventure)

God's Broken Man
(Allan Brooks) (Christian Fiction)

Myrtle Beach Murder
(Allan Brooks)(Christian Fiction)

Fall of Fort Fisher
(Juvenile action/adventure)
(Civil War)

Andrew's War
(Juvenile action/adventure)
(Civil War)

Fighting Marines: Hardy's Commission

Fighting Marines: Hardy's Challenge

Donland's Courage
(Tenth Book in Series)

Chapter One

"Be dark enough in an hour," Jackson said and spat a stream of tobacco juice over the railing.

"Aye," Ashcroft agreed.

"Best keep a close eye on Haskins when we've finished. He'll pilfer any liquor he finds and be drunk before you know he'd had a nip or two," Jackson advised.

"Aye, and thank you for telling me. I'd not want his like to make a mess of it. Captain Donland would not thank me for it," Ashcroft said.

"Jones and Little are more steady than the others. I'd have them in the lead beside you," Jackson suggested.

Ashcroft said nothing.

Jackson spat his wad over the railing and moved away. He'd done what he could to help the young lieutenant. More'n he should have done. A cutting out party in the black of night was not an easy task even for a seasoned man. It would have made more sense for the captain to leave Ashcroft aboard and go himself. It wasn't like him to send an untried man to do a task such as this.

An hour passed, the night was black without the moon. "Mr. Jackson put the boats over if you please," Donland said softly.

He ordered the ship as quiet as possible. The success of the cutting out operation depended on complete surprise. Should the men, just inland of the beach, hear something and feel threatened, they would be away and upriver in minutes. Donland had no desire to give chase.

The boats went over the side without making a splash. Overhead, faint stars showed through the thin clouds. The moon would rise in another two hours. The operation had to be complete before then or men would die needlessly.

"Mr. Jackson, the gig too, if you please," Donland said.

"Aye, Captain," Jackson answered and asked, "Will you be sending another party across?"

"Aye, three men," Donland answered but did not explain.

Jackson did as ordered. He knew Donland well enough to know his captain and two others would be going ashore. The purpose would wait. He felt better knowing the captain did not intend to leave all resting on Ashcroft's shoulders.

"Mr. Ashcroft, keep those men quiet!" Jackson snapped.

Several minutes passed before David came alongside of Jackson and said, "The Captain's compliments Mr. Jackson, he'd see you below."

"Aye," Jackson replied.

Jackson was surprised to find Donland dressed in clothes from the slop chest. Honest was likewise dressed.

"Mr. Dewitt will have the watch while we are away. He is to continue to lie-to and wait for our return. Honest, Bill Freedman and myself are going across. It is my intention to subdue any watchers or fisherman. Once we have accomplished that task, if it is necessary, we will locate a footpath for Mr. Ashcroft's party.

The plan is not changed, Mr. Ashcroft will cut off escape and your party will subdue the camp," Donland said as he shoved his sword into his pants.

"What if there are more than two or three on the beach?" Jackson asked.

"Then we will return before you are to leave," Donland answered. "As I said, this must be done quickly and without great risk to our people. It would serve no good to lose good men on a venture of little value."

"Aye," Jackson agreed.

Bill and Honest piloted the gig smoothly across the calm sea. The bulk of the swells were blocked by the sandbank jutting out and along the beach at low tide. Donland stood holding a cast net. To all appearances, they were three men fishing in the shallows.

"Pass that jug!" Donland said loudly.

"You've had your share!" Honest said back to Donland.

"No more'n you, give it!" Donland said and snatched up the jug and drank. Putting the jug down he said loudly, "Put in over there, I've got to piss!"

Bill and Honest obeyed and ran the gig onto the beach. Donland stepped over the gunnel and made as if he were undoing buttons. Honest and Bill both stood and stretched, then stepped on to the sand. They saw no one; there was a faint smell of tobacco smoke in the air.

Donland said in a whisper, "Follow me, pretend you are drunk."

They obeyed and followed him to the trees. He drew his sword, and they did likewise. Bill tugged at Donland's sleeve, "man," he said, and took Donland's arm and used it to point to a place just inland.

"Aye," Donland whispered. "You go along the edge, we'll come round."

He watched Bill disappear. If there were only one man, Bill would dispatch him. If more, they would soon know.

Donland and Honest moved quietly through the sand and around clumps of trees and brush. There were three men; two appeared to be sleeping while the third stood propped against a tree. It was too dark to see weapons and were it not for the men's white faces they wouldn't have been seen.

"Boots Captain," Honest whispered.

Donland removed his boots but kept his socks on. What was to be done had to be done quickly and silently. The scrunch of sand under his boot would give away their location.

"Bill?" Donland asked in a whisper.

"He'll see us and move when we do," Honest whispered.

They crept within six feet of the closest man sleeping.

"I'll take the one standing, you take the sleepers," Donland whispered.

"Aye," Honest said.

Donland shot from a crouch across the small clearing toward the standing man. Just as he slashed down with his sword his foot hung on a root. The tip of the blade ripped across the man's throat and blood spewed as if from a fountain. The man clutched his throat to stem the flow and sank to his knees. Donland landed on top of the man, rolled to one side as he tried to bring up his sword for another blow. Bill landed on the man and drove his knife into the man's chest.

Donland turned and was relieved to see Honest standing over one of the sleeping men. He had knifed the man through one eye. No doubt he hacked the other's throat, for there had been no sound.

"Quickly done," Donland said in a soft voice. "Let us find a footpath or trail. Our men will be coming across soon. Bill, you take the lead for your eyesight in this black is better than mine."

"Aye, Captain," Bill said and moved toward the brush.

It was as Donland suspected; there was a game trail parallel to the river that meandered inland. Further along was the footpath the smugglers were using that ran along the bank of the river.

They came within earshot of the smuggler's camp. "I'll go forward, you remain here," Donland said.

Through the brush he glimpsed a small fire. Men were sprawled on the ground sleeping. The whiteness of furled sails caught his attention. He was pleased that the coastal trader was still anchored in the river. It was of no value and he would burn it after capturing the munitions the smugglers had offloaded. He estimated there were twenty or more men.

Slipping quietly back to where Honest and Bill waited, he made his decision. "Bill and I will stay here. Honest you go back to the beach and fetch Mr. Ashcroft. Have him set two men to watch over the watchers camp. The rebels may send someone to relieve those men."

"Aye," Honest replied and slipped silently away.

Fifteen minutes more or less passed before Honest returned, followed by Ashcroft and his party. The young lieutenant's round face was pale, like a beacon. Being red-haired and freckled-faced, Ashcroft tanned very little.

"Spread your men out along the path," Donland whispered. "Once they are in place, we will wait for the signal from Mr. Jackson."

"Aye, Captain," Ashcroft answered.

Jackson's signal, the hoot of an owl, came moments after Ashcroft had moved away.

"We've no time," Donland said to Honest.

Honest returned the hoot with a poor imitation.

"At em' men!" Donland shouted and set off in a run toward the first man he saw.

The sleeping men were slow to rouse, but one of the guards turned when hearing Donland's voice. A pistol shot rang out, catching the man in the chest. He died in the light of the campfire.

From the river came shouts as men boarded the trader and others stormed forward from the riverbank. Pistols banged and men screamed. The heavy night air filled with the clang of swords and the gurgle of dying men.

One man rose up from near Donland and lashed out with a sword, his blade catching only Donland's shirttail. Donland pivoted to his right and brought his blade down on the man's shoulder. He felt the jar of the blade on bone. The man screamed and dropped his sword. Donland turned away to meet his next foe. There was none. It was over.

"Mr. Jackson, what of our men?" Donland asked as he surveyed the camp.

"Six of our company wounded, they'll mend in a day or two. Can't say the same for that lot," Jackson said as he nodded toward the camp. "Thirty either dead or dying, four prisoners."

Ashcroft strode up to Donland and Jackson. "I've secured the weapons and set a guard onboard the boat."

"Well done, Mr. Ashcroft," Donland commended the young man. "We will take stock of our capture when daylight comes."

"Aye, and thank you, captain," Ashcroft said.

"Mr. Jackson gather your men and return to *Hornet*, Mr. Ashcroft and I, with his men, will remain for the night."

"Aye Captain. Shall we bring *Hornet* closer, inshore?"

"I think not Mr. Jackson, we've no knowledge of what might lie up river. Double the watch, just in case someone is about who considers *Hornet* vulnerable while we are ashore."

"Aye, Captain," Jackson answered.

"And Jackson, inspect the men on the beach. There was a goodly amount of spirits among those we dispatched, I'd not want any taken aboard."

"Aye, Captain, aye," Jackson answered.

The munitions and supplies seized at the river camp were enough to outfit a company or more. Sumerford had told Donland that the rebels were arming in preparation of raising an attack against Savannah once the French arrived. Donland asked what information had been received concerning the French and Sumerford had merely said, *scant*.

"However, I am privy to communications between the French and the colonials. Seems they are pressuring the French to take Savannah. And, I believe the capture of the munitions and supplies add weight to the fact that those preparations are underway."

Chapter Two

Donland awoke to the singing of birds. He lay still listening for several long minutes, enjoying the songs of the birds. The sun shone through the window warming face causing him to feel at peace with the world. The bed was soft; the sheets clean and freshly ironed. The smells of ship and sea were a distant memory. He lay drinking in all the joy of being alive and on land.

A light tapping at the door interrupted the peace of his soul.

"Your breakfast, Mr. Donland," an unfamiliar voice called from the other side of the door.

"Enter!" he called.

The door opened without a sound. A tall black man dressed in the livery of a servant entered silently. He held a covered silver tray. The servant placed the tray on the small table near the window. "Coffee is hot Mr. Donland, so take care."

"Aye!" Donland replied.

The man lifted the lid off the tray and the smell of coffee floated immediately to Donland's nose. It was a delicious smell, one that warmed the soul.

"There's bacon, sausage, eggs and grits sir. Some blackberry jam for your biscuits."

Donland's mouth watered as he slipped to the side of the bed and sat up. "Thank you," he managed.

"Can I get you anything else, Mr. Donland?" the servant asked.

"No, no, this is more than sufficient," Donland said as his mind was completely on the food. He had forgotten he was naked. The nightshirt that had been provided was too heavy for the hot night.

"Sir there is a robe at the foot of the bed," the servant reminded.

Donland stood and picked up the robe and slipped it on.

The servant began pouring coffee, "I thought you might enjoy a glass of fresh apple juice."

Apple juice! He had loved apple juice and apple cider as a boy. He'd not tasted it since coming aboard his first ship.

"Thank you," Donland said with delight.

Grits swimming in butter had become one of his favorite foods. He remembered the first time he was served a bowl of grits and questioned if grits were a type of rice. No, the person had answered; grits are made from corn.

The blackberry jam was another childhood memory. One of fall days with golden and red leaves. The thought conjured up another lost memory of maple syrup on hot, freshly baked bread. The mental image of his mother smiling at him brought a pang of loss. He'd not thought of her in years. He shook his head to put her from his mind and picked up the cup of coffee. It was the best he had ever tasted.

He ate with total abandonment, thinking of nothing but the food. To his amazement, he finished the whole breakfast and still desired more. Standing, he went to the window. On the street below, a carriage passed. Other carriages were visible in front of the small framed Catholic church, he assumed the owners were inside attending morning mass. Another carriage came into view; there was no mistaking Sumerford as he exited the carriage.

A light tap on the door caused him to turn. "Enter," he called.

The servant came in bearing a pitcher on a tray, towels and a razor. "If you are ready sir, I will shave you." he said. A maid appeared and swept up the breakfast tray. She departed without a word.

"Yes, yes, quite ready," Donland said.

The servant placed the tray on the table where the maid had removed the breakfast tray. Donland sat. Neither spoke as the servant lathered Donland's face. The man had a still and steady hand. The razor was honed so fine that Donland scarcely felt it on his skin.

The maid tapped at the door and entered without being bidden to do so. She carried Donland's freshly laundered and ironed uniform to the bed and carefully laid each item out. "Elias will bring your boots, sir," she said and left.

The shave was quickly completed. The servant produced a pair of scissors and began trimming Donland's hair. All the while he worked he did not speak.

Another tap at the door and a boy of no more than twelve entered bearing the freshly shined boots. He sat the boots beside the bed and left without speaking.

The servant put away the scissors and removed the towel from Donland's neck. "Shall I help you dress?" he asked.

"No, but thank you. I shall manage."

The servant picked up the tray and went to the door.

Sumerford was waiting in the sitting room. He wore a fine light tan frock coat with tails, calf length tan boots, white ruffled shirt with an ivory colored neckerchief. In his hand was a simple black hat with a small white cockade. "I've a carriage outside," he announced.

Donland felt quite ordinary in his uniform, even though it was well starched and heavily creased with a flat iron. He could not picture himself wearing such as Sumerford wore.

"Our first stop is the tailor. I would think something a bit modern for you and not as stuffy as that uniform," Sumerford said.

Donland said simply, "I think not."

"Dear Isaac, you can't be seen at social gatherings in that. Were you a post captain with a chest full of medals, you could manage. But a mere lieutenant's uniform, it will not do."

"Mathias, I've no need of such as you have and I've no intention of spending half my nights in the company of politicians and merchants."

Sumerford laughed. He shook his head with unbelief. "You sound like the drunkard in the gutter refusing a bath and a clean shirt. Friend, I may not make a silk purse from a sow's ear, but I can present a naval officer as a gentleman. And as to your seeing no purpose in it, I remind you that Betty will be arriving tomorrow. She may love your rough salty hide, but she will expect to be on your arm in the evenings among those politicians and merchants."

Donland knew his friend was right. Betty Sumerford of Boston would be in demand.

The tailor's shop reminded Donland of a chandler's shop more than it did a place of fancy clothes. Bolts of cloth, spools of yarns and threads and assorted trays of ribbon were scattered about haphazardly. Wire-framed torsos of men and women of all sizes, either partially dressed or undressed, were arranged along one wall. The smell of the place was a heavy mixture of dyes and new cloth.

The tailor, Mr. Braxton, was tall and thin. He moved like a stork. His assistants, mostly blacks, were busy sewing various garments. Donland assumed they were slaves.

"Gentlemen, how may I assist you?" Braxton asked.

"My friend is in need of evening wear and daywear," Sumerford said.

"Daywear such as yours?" Braxton asked.

Sumerford smiled. "A little more modest would suit his tastes and comfort," Sumerford answered.

Donland was pleased that Mathias knew him well enough to know he had no desire to be dressed as a peacock.

"And a new uniform," Donland added.

"Cotton or wool for the uniform?" Braxton asked.

"Cotton, I would suggest," Sumerford said.

To Donland he said, "You may be in Savannah often."

Braxton and a male assistant measured Donland while Sumerford sat in a chair and smoked one of his little black cigars.

Donland felt ill at ease with all the prodding and pushing. He understood how a servant girl in an alehouse must feel on a nightly basis. Perhaps Braxton enjoyed fitting his female clientele. It could be enjoyable work.

"I will return to *Hornet* for the afternoon," Donland said as they were leaving the tailor shop.

Sumerford faced Donland, "But, dear fellow, it's not quite noon. Let us have some boiled shrimp and rice, a good bottle of wine and a cigar or two. The is no need to rush."

Donland replied, "There are the day-to-day duties that require my attention. I've had enough breakfast that I shall not want for another morsel until this evening. I fear I would be poor company until I've seen to my duties."

"If you must, then so be it. At least I can offer you a ride to the docks."

"Thank you, but no. I need to stretch my legs and I need to roust out Jackson wherever he may have passed the evening."

Sumerford nodded. "That may be so," he paused and asked, "tonight at seven?"

"Aye, that would do me well."

Of Jackson, there was no sign. Donland looked in on a few drinking establishments, but neither Jackson nor others from *Hornet* were present. He thought nothing of not seeing Jackson and assumed he was either back aboard or had gone across to the island.

Hornet was anchored off the tip of Fig Island. The anchorage was chosen that the men might frequent the island's taverns and the brothels rather than Savannah proper. It would do them good to be ashore and away from the rigors of ship discipline.

The gig was not at the dock were he left it. Jackson must have taken it and not yet sent it back across. No matter, he spied a bumboat with two young women sitting at the oars.

"For hire?" he asked.

"Yes, but the boat only," the plumb girl responded.

"Very good, it is all I seek. The sloop yonder," he pointed.

"Four pennies," the plump girl stated.

"One!" Donland said firmly.

"Find another boat!"

"That I can do easy enough."

"Three!" the skinny girl said and drew a mean look from the plump girl.

"Two!" Donland said flatly.

"Agreed," the skinny girl answered.

Donland climbed down into the boat.

The boat was surprisingly clean. Donland seated himself in the stern. The two girls, each no more than sixteen by his guess, sat facing him. He stared past them, averting his eyes from the plump girl's rising and falling breasts.

13

The girls skillfully maneuvered the boat along *Hornet's* hull. The gig was not present; perhaps Jackson had not come aboard as he thought. He took two pennies from his pocket, thought better of it and added a third. If he were to need their services, again they would be more than willing.

Ashcroft, Dawkins and David stood together as Donland came over the side. They saluted and Donland returned their salutes, then doffed his hat.

"I take it Mr. Jackson is not aboard."

"He has not come aboard Captain," Ashcroft answered.

"The gig was not at the dock," Donland said.

"It has not returned, I assumed it and the crew were at your disposal," Ashcroft replied.

Donland noted that the larger of *Hornet's* boats was also away. "Are others ashore?" he asked.

Ashcroft appeared uncomfortable but answered," Aye sir, Mr. Dewitt and two dozen went across to the island at dawn."

Donland made a mental note that no more than a dozen men were on deck. None were doing any work. The deck was tidy, lines were coiled, all sails neatly furled. It was evident that, in all respects, *Hornet* was not neglected.

Donland could see no fault and said, "Let us go below Mr. Ashcroft."

A good number of men were in their hammocks and those not were playing cards or tending personal tasks. All ceased talking when they realized their captain was present. Donland merely nodded to those who met his eyes. He said nothing as he made his way forward and back again. Ashcroft followed a step behind.

Donland removed his hat as he entered his cabin. He expected Honest to appear, but he did not.

"Mr. Dewitt took Honest with him. I assume he thought he would need support should a man become difficult," Ashcroft said, anticipating Donland's question.

"Wise on his part," Donland acknowledged.

Donland unbuttoned his coat and draped it over the back of a chair. He then sat at his desk, eyed the papers and logs and asked, "Anything to report?"

"No, Captain. We've no signals, visitors or difficulties. The bilge has been pumped and the stores checked. All is in proper order."

"Thank you, Mr. Ashcroft. That will be all."

After Ashcroft went out, Donland went to the locker and removed a bottle of wine and a glass. There was a knock at the door.

"Enter!" he called.

David came in. "Beg pardon sir, but will you be going across to the town in the evening?"

"Aye," Donland answered while running his finger along a line of figures in the log.

"I would be ever so grateful, sir, to accompany you."

"For what purpose?" Donland looked up and asked.

The boy's face showed uncertainty, but he managed, "I should like to see a bit of the town."

"Are you going alone?"

"Aye sir, Simon is with Honest on the island. I've no one else."

Donland considered the request. He would not be returning until morning, and David would be on his own without a way to return. He thought of the two girls with the bumboat and rejected the possibility.

"Perhaps it would be best for you to wait until Simon can go with you."

Disappointment was on David's face. Seeing it Donland smiled broadly and said, "If not tonight surely tomorrow for Miss Sumerford arrives tomorrow and I'm certain she will want to see you."

David's face lit up with joy.

Donland continued, "We will dine with her tomorrow evening."

"Oh, sir, that is wonderful news."

"I thought you might be pleased. Of course there will be others, so you will need to have your uniform cleaned and boots shined. Have you a decent shirt?"

David was silent, then answered, "I've not."

Donland smiled, "Then you have a purpose for going across to the town. Let us decide after the boats return. If they do not before it is time for me to leave, I will consider other arrangements for you."

"Thank you, sir, thank you," David said.

"See to your duties, Mr. Welles."

Dewitt and Honest returned early afternoon. Several of the men were so drunk they had to be carried aboard. One was unconscious, and Donland noticed a rather large knot on the man's forehead and a blackened eye.

"Fell down, Captain," Honest stated.

Donland thought, "with help" but did not say it.

Jackson still had not returned. Donland was concerned. He would have to see what or who was detaining his first officer.

"Mr. Ashcroft detail a fresh crew for the launch," Donland ordered. "Mr. Welles and Honest will accompany me ashore. They will be returning this evening."

Donland was not surprised to see Simon Vickers sitting beside David in the launch. As the youngest of the boys aboard *Hornet,* they had little choice but to be each other's friend. He felt better about David seeing the town with Simon to accompany him.

"Give way all!" Donland ordered.

There were two merchantmen at the quay being loaded with bales of cotton. Donland had no doubt they would be bound for the mills in England and then return with finished cloth. The colonies for all their bluster and brashness were still dependent on England for trade. That he knew would continue long after the rebellion ended. Trade was the lifeblood of all nations and none dared to alienate markets. The moneymen would not tolerate such, no matter the politics.

They reached the dock in a matter of minutes. Donland was first out of the launch, as was his right as captain. He waited as the launch was secured and for the crew to climb onto the dock before giving instructions.

"Anderson divide the men into two parties. One to go south along the river and one to go north. Check for our gig and the crew. When you find the crew, inquire after Mr. Jackson. Once you find him, give him my compliments and to report to me at Wolseley's on Bull Street."

"Aye, aye captain," Anderson answered.

Donland turned his attention to Honest. "Take the boys to the tailor shop on Jefferson Street. Purchase new britches and two new shirts for Mr. Welles. Have it set down on my account."

"Aye, Captain," Honest answered.

"Once you have completed that task, seek out Anderson and assist him if necessary. Mr. Welles and Simon may take in the sights if you have no objections."

"None, sir, and I will attend the other matters," Honest answered.

Sumerford arrived at the restaurant shortly after Donland's arrival. He wore black attire befitting a funeral.

"Whose wake did you attend?" Donland asked.

Sumerford smiled a tight smile and replied, "An astute description of the affair. Such was the meeting with the army and local hacks; my role, however, was simply perfunctory."

"Gathering gossip is more like it."

Again the tight smile, but no reply.

"Ah, mmm. Shall we dine?" Donland asked.

"Yes, yes, let us do," Sumerford said.

They were shown a table in a small room containing four tables. Two of the tables were occupied with older couples, the others unoccupied. A chandelier hung above provided a good amount of light. The servant seated them and then poured red wine into two delicate stemmed glasses. The table was set with highly polished fine silver.

"Let us begin with a serving of chilled shrimp," Sumerford suggested.

"Aye," Donland answered.

They were midway in their meal of roast lamb with mushroom wine sauce when David entered. He saw Donland and hurried over, causing heads to turn.

Donland observed his entry but was not alarmed.

David had the forethought to remove his hat and carried it cradled in his arm. He saluted, then bent low to Donland's ear. "Mr. Jackson is gravely wounded, sir. You should come."

Donland merely nodded. He leaned across the table and said, "I beg your leave Mr. Sumerford. Mr. Jackson has been injured."

Sumerford did not hesitate. "I shall accompany you," he said and rose.

Sumerford pulled his card from a pocket and placed it in the center of the table. The proprietor would prepare a bill for the meal and send it around to the address on the card.

"Where is he?" Donland asked once they were outside.

David answered, "Honest is with him. They are taking him to the ship."

Sumerford suggested, "Let us go to the dock and intercept them. I've an acquaintance that is a more than an able physician. I would think your man would receive better care from him."

"Very good of you to offer, I would prefer him over what can be done aboard ship," Donland said.

Sumerford signaled, and a carriage came alongside. "To the Montgomery Street dock," he instructed the driver.

Donland asked David, "What happened, do you know?"

David answered with concern in his voice, "Honest said he was either set on by robbers or he had a fight. He didn't know which because Mr. Jackson was in an alley and covered over with filth like someone tried to hide him."

"What of his injuries?" Donland asked.

"Three stab wounds and several cuts on his hands and arms. He wasn't talking while I was there."

The carriage arrived at the dock and Donland recognized his men gathered in a small knot. They separated as he approached.

"Mr. Jackson?" he asked.

The short man named Duffy stepped forward. "In the gig, Captain. They're making for the ship."

Donland looked past the men. He saw a moving lantern and assumed it was the gig. "Ahoy! *Hornet!*" he shouted.

The gig continued without slowing. Donland shouted again and waved his arms.

A shot rang out. Donland turned. Sumerford had fired a pistol into the air.

"Ahoy *Hornet!*" Donland shouted again.

Someone in the gig either heard him or recognized him. The man shouted something but it was lost on the wind.

The boat sat still then turned toward the dock. As it drew near he recognized the gig's crew and Honest sitting in the stern.

Sumerford took charge once the boat reached the dock. "Into the carriage, there's a doctor two blocks from here, a good one."

Donland did not argue. There was no one aboard *Hornet* save the witch doctor to attend Jackson.

Chapter Three

The doctor was a young man of no more than thirty, slight in frame and bearded. He examined Jackson's wounds, cut away some flesh, stitched the deeper wounds, applied a strong smelling salve of camphor and dressed the wounds with neat bandaging.

"I've done what can be done. The rest is not in my hands," the doctor stated.

"How long before he can return to duty?" Donland asked.

"Duty!" the doctor exclaimed. "Captain he shall do well to make it through the night. I'd not give odds of him living beyond sunset tomorrow."

"Surely he has a chance?" Donland blurted.

"Yes, a chance but a slim chance Captain Donland. The wounds in his chest are deep and one has punctured a lung. You probably noticed the blood on his lips and the sucking sound as he breathes."

"Aye," Donland answered.

"The strongest of men would have little hope of living and if one should, he'd be an invalid with only a short time remaining to him."

The doctor's words shook Donland to his core. Jackson was more than his first officer. They had fought together, eaten together, drank together received promotions together and so much more. They were friends and brothers. Jackson was his strengthen when he had none.

He remembered the day they came aboard *Medusa*, he as second lieutenant and Jackson as master's mate. They were no more than acquaintances aboard ship but that changed when they were to deliver the *Morgador* to the prize court. Donland remembered the thrill and the burden of that first command. Were it not for Jackson, the venture would have failed. The shared experiences on the island while repairing *Morgador* had drawn them as close as brothers. *Hornet* would not be the same without him. The man was as strong as an ox, wise beyond his years and a leader of men. He was irreplaceable.

"What can I do?" Donland asked.

"As I've said, his life is not in my hands nor is it in yours. If you are a praying man, pray," the doctor answered.

Sumerford placed a hand on Donland's shoulder. "I'll not require you further this evening," Sumerford said. "Remain with him and I shall call before noon."

"Aye," Donland acknowledged.

Sumerford faced the doctor. "Doctor Addison I would that you remain as long as necessary. I shall be responsible for your fee and will more than compensate you for your efforts."

"I shall," Addison answered and turned back to Jackson.

Prayer was all Donland had, and he exerted himself on Jackson's behalf. Doctor Addison did as he promised and did not leave Jackson's bedside. Every few minutes Addison dipped a cloth into a bowl of water and wet Jackson's lips. He explained to Donland that he had found that his patients struggled less to swallow if their lips are moistened. From Jackson, there was an occasional gurgle of the throat but no movement.

Sunrise dispelled the gloom of the night and signaled hope as Jackson croaked and licked his lips.

Donland rose from his chair, "Doctor?"

"A good sign but only a sign," Addison said more to himself than to Donland.

To Donland he said, "The fever will only grow. If it should peak and break, he might live. But, as I told you last night, he'll never be the man he was. Such wounds shorten a man's days."

Donland nodded, he understood, Jackson's days at sea as a ship's officer were over.

A tap at the door drew Donland's attention. A very tall servant entered holding a large tray. A young woman bearing a smaller tray with a coffee service followed him. "Your breakfast sir," the tall man stated.

Donland had not considered hunger or thirst during the night.

"Aye," he said.

The servant lifted the coverings to display eggs, ham, sausage, Johnnycakes, assorted fruits and biscuits."

"More than enough," Donland stated.

Donland glanced at Jackson there was no recognition of the food. Were he himself, he would be beaming with delight.

"Let us eat," Addison said. "There's naught we can do." He crossed to the sideboard and began to fill a plate.

"Jackson would make quick work of this tray," Donland mused.

"And, he might again," Addison replied.

The words were the first positive ones from the doctor. Donland cocked an eye. "He might again?"

"Not to get your hopes up Captain but he is far better than I dared expect after passing the night. There is the battle with infection to be fought and as I said, should he win that, then he might live."

The gloom in Donland's heart was nonetheless lifted. He felt he could eat and enjoy the meal.

"I've eaten my fill and I've done all I can for your man. I'll take my leave and return before nightfall. I've other patients in need of my attention. Captain you can rest assured that he will be no better and no worse if I stay by his side."

Donland nodded. "I understand Doctor. I shall continue to moisten his lips and tend to him as I can. Should the dressing be adjusted or changed?"

"No, the bleeding has stopped and I will change the dressings when I return."

Just as the doctor was leaving Honest entered with his son.

"Has he come to sir?" Honest inquired.

"No, not as yet. The doctor said he would not until the fever has swelled and dissipated. Even then Jackson may not live."

"Aye, I've seen more than one man die after the fever has left him."

Donland wet Jackson's lips.

"Shall I tend him?" Honest asked.

"Aye, your efforts will be far greater than mine," Donland answered.

As Honest sat in the chair beside the bed he said, "With your permission I'll send Simon back across and fetch Baako."

"The witch-doctor?"

"Aye Captain, the men swear he is as good if not better than any surgeon."

Donland considered and said, "Very well, let us give Jackson every benefit we may give. Is the gig still at the quay?"

"Aye, sir."

23

"Very well, I will go with Simon to the dock and instruct the gig's crew to take him across."

He turned to the boy, "Simon, you will inform Baako that Mr. Jackson has been stabbed in the chest, a lung was punctured. Have him bring anything that he thinks will help Mr. Jackson heal."

"Aye, Captain," Simon answered.

Donland mused, "Doctor Addison may not appreciate my giving a witch-doctor charge of his patient."

Honest allowed himself a small chuckle. "I say not Sir."

Sumerford arrived minutes after Simon's departure. He wore a sky-blue coat, bright blue breeches, bright blue waistcoat and white stockings. His hat was the color of his coat with a peacock feather.

"We've an appointment with the governor, Sir James Wright. I would suggest you return to your room, bathe and dress. I will call for you at a quarter of one."

Donland was hesitant to leave. "Is it important that I attend?"

"Yes, I have information to share with the governor concerning French and colonial troops and ship movements. You, being a naval officer understand better than I, the blockading of harbors. Your voice may sway the argument."

Donland heard Sumerford but wasn't clear what was asked of him. "Blockading harbors?" he asked.

"Yes, but I'm not at liberty to say anything more as in these times all walls have ears."

Donland understood. The details of the conversation they were to have with the governor would be shared once they were en route to the governor.

"Do you intend to leave Honest with Jackson?" Sumerford asked.

"Aye, and others also. Doctor Addison said he would return before nightfall. It is his opinion that all that can be done was done. I've a man aboard *Hornet* who has achieved good results with natural medications."

"A witch doctor?" Sumerford asked.

Donland grinned, "Aye."

"You're not grasping at straws I trust?"

"A drowning man takes whatever help is at hand be it a straw or a well tossed line. My father said in a sermon, 'only a fool turns away salvation' and I have found the saying to serve me well. Salvation can come at the hand of an uneducated man as easily as it can come from an educated man."

"That I can agree on," Sumerford said. "Let us attend the Governor."

Governor Wright remained seated as Sumerford and Donland entered. "Gentlemen," he greeted.

Sumerford, without invitation, sat in one of the straight-backed wooden chairs in front of Wright's desk. "Sir James I've asked for this audience to warn you of French intentions to take Savannah. My information is from reliable sources that are aware of communications between the French Admiral D'estang and General Lincoln."

"A rumor?" Wright inquired.

"Hardly Sir James, I have copies of the exchanges and in them D'estang is enthusiastic concerning the venture. He has the force to accomplish the task, some thirty ships-of-line and more than five thousand troops. Lincoln is to provide upward of three thousand colonial troops."

Wright held up a hand. "Mr. Sumerford my commanders have no such intelligence. Colonel Campbell dispatched Ashe's army at Briar Creek. The colonials don't have a force of any size left in Georgia. As to Lincoln, he is still licking his wounds in Charleston and his force is made up of mostly untrained and ill-equipped farmers. Therefore, I take little countenance in your warning."

Sumerford twisted in his chair toward Donland. "Captain Donland what of Admiral D'estang's fleet?"

"Formable," Donland answered. "I was on station during the battle at Grenada. His ships-of-line out numbered Lord Byron, and he was able to inflict considerable damage. In turn, he received his due share. Given these weeks since the battle, Admiral D'estang will have set to right his damage. Lord Byron has returned with his fleet to England. We have little left to stand against D'estang if he decides to take Savannah. I can attest to Mr. Sumerford's information for at Grenada D'estang had several large troop transports with four thousand troops aboard. He has the force to blockade the approaches to Savannah and to lay siege."

Donland was about to add more but Governor Wright held up a hand signaling him to stop.

"Be that as it may Lieutenant, until you can bring me information of an imminent threat, I have many other pressing matters to attend. I suggest you gentlemen continue to be alert and if Admiral D'estang sails with confirmed intent to do us harm, then inform me. Until then, I see no need to take any action. Good day gentlemen."

Sumerford rose from the chair. "As you wish Sir James, as you wish."

Sumerford sat back in the carriage and pulled one of his foul smelling cigarillos from the case. As he lit it he said, "As I thought, Wright is a short-sighted bureaucrat. A capable man by all accounts but is happy to be bound by the immediate rather than the expedient. We've no choice therefore, but to do as he requests. We will confirm and report. Doing such may well entail our running from the French with our tails tucked between our legs so to speak."

"Are you suggesting we seek out the French fleet and be the fox to their hounds?" Donland asked.

"Are you up to the task?" Sumerford asked as he lit his cigarillo.

"I am under your orders," Donland answered.

"So you are old son, so you are."

A foul stench greeted Donland as he entered Jackson's room. His friend lay as he had when Donland had left him. The bandages covering Jackson's chest were gone and replaced with a blackish slathering of salve. Baako rose from a squatted position near the window.

"How is he Baako?" Donland asked.

"Bad but be good," Baako answered in his broken English.

Donland nodded. It occurred to him that the witch-doctor was more optimistic than the doctor was.

"When?" he asked.

Baako held up three fingers.

"Three days?" Donland asked.

"Aye Captain," Baako answered with a huge grin.

Donland leaned and patted Jackson arm. "God hasn't finished with you yet nor I. Mind you, I've work for you," he said and straightened.

"Aye Captain," Baako said and his face contorted as he sought words. "Food... ah... no rum but burn," he managed and rubbed his belly.

"You need food for Mr. Jackson?" Donland asked.

"Aye Captain," Baako said then added, "no rum but burn." He put a finger to his lips and drew a line downward to his stomach. "Much burn."

Donland considered what the man was trying to say. "Drink that burns?" he asked.

"Aye Captain," Baako said excitedly.

Instantly Donland said, "brandy."

Baako's face twisted to show he did not understand.

27

"Whisky?" Donland said.

Baako beamed.

"Whiskey for Mr. Jackson?" he asked

"Aye Captain."

"You shall have it. I'll send someone to you with food and whiskey."

Donland left Jackson's room feeling much better about Jackson. He had no idea what Baako would do with the whiskey or what Doctor Addison would have say about Baako's ministrations. He could only hope Jackson would improve in the few hours before Doctor Addison's arrival.

A note from Sumerford lay on the sideboard in Donland's room. "Dinner with Betty will be at eight. Dress like a gentleman and I will call at seven-thirty."

He had five hours to prepare, more than enough time to return to *Hornet*.

Once aboard, there were matters to consider; preparations to make and to do so he needed a deck under his heels. Sumerford, no doubt, planned a voyage to ascertain the French admiral's intentions. To spy on the French fleet would place *Hornet* in peril. Without a steady first officer such as Jackson the peril would be increased.

Ashcroft leaned forward in his chair and answered Donland's question. "Aye Sir, we are ready to sail. I took the liberty of sending Mr. Jones ashore earlier to replenish stores and water. Our company is still short eleven men as I've not been able to secure replacements. Mr. Aldridge has seen to accounting for all cordage and spares. He reports all has been checked for rot and condition. We've no shortage."

"Very good Mr. Ashcroft. We may have a day or two to seek men to fill out our company. Tomorrow I will go around and visit with the provost. That is if we do not sail before then.

Our, Mr. Sumerford may at this minute be planning our departure."

"Aye Sir," Ashcroft said thoughtfully.

Donland stood. "Keep our company aboard. I'd not chance any running afoul of the provost or falling victim to accidents."

"What of Mr. Jackson?" Ashcroft asked.

"Doctor Addison holds out little hope but our Baako is more hopeful."

"I take it then that if we sail Mr. Jackson will remain ashore."

"Aye, you will be acting first lieutenant until Mr. Jackson returns to duty."

Ashcroft's face showed no emotion. "I'll draw up the watch list."

"Aye," Donland replied.

Chapter Four

Donland was dressed in his new finery and waited in front of the house he was staying. His back was already wet with sweat. The sun was low on the horizon but the humidity and heat of Savannah would continue until midnight. The lack of wind or breeze was one of the things Donland did not like about being ashore.

David wore his midshipman's coat, new britches and a new shirt. The boy's hat was shabby.

"You may carry your hat if you wish," Donland said.

"Sir?" David said questioning.

"Your hat is worse for wear. Better if you tucked it in your arm."

David removed his hat.

Donland smiled at the boy.

Sumerford arrived in an open carriage. He was dressed in a royal blue suit and was alone.

"Let us be off," Sumerford said in greeting. "The house is five miles in the country."

"Aye," Donland agreed and stepped into the carriage followed by David. He had expected to be dining at a local inn.

Sumerford clarified, "The house is that of a family friend. We'll not be disturbed."

Once they were clear of the city traffic, the carriage driver brought the horse to a trot. The brisk pace was a welcome relief as it created a slight breeze.

"Much better don't you agree?" Sumerford asked.

"Aye," Donland answered.

The horse covered the distance quickly. The house was not large; it was a modest two-story home with a porch across the front. There were no ornate towering columns. Large oak trees grew close to the frame house covered with a gray slate roof. Limbs hung over most of the roof. Certainly not the grand country estate Donland was expecting. There were four carriages in front of the house.

A servant was waiting and escorted Donland and Sumerford into the house.

The house was surprisingly cool. The wide hall in which they stood was open at each end and a fresh breeze flowed. From one of the rooms came the music of banjo and guitar.

The servant stopped at the first door. Inside Donland saw Betty standing with a glass in hand talking with two men, one very tall wearing a lieutenant's uniform that hung as if it were on a skeleton and the other a ram-rod straight backed man of middle-age. She turned, saw him and smiled. He hurried to her and embraced. David followed at his heels.

"Oh Isaac, I have missed you so," she said into his ear.

"Aye, and I you."

Betty released Donland and turned her attention to David.

"My how handsome you are," she said and beamed.

Sumerford joined them and gave her a sisterly hug.

Stepping away from Betty, Sumerford introduced the two men, "Colonel John Maitland commander of the 71st Highland currently bivouacked at Beaufort. And, this is Lieutenant Harrison Morse lately of the *Lion*."

Donland was instantly alert. A mere lieutenant did not just happen to appear in Sumerford's company.

"The table is set, let us go in," Sumerford said to the little group.

The dining room was small with large open windows on two sides. The room was hot and seated a dozen comfortably. Donland sat next to Betty and Lieutenant Morse sat opposite him. David was seated at the end of the table.

Glass pitchers of water on the table condensed and ran down the sides of the glass. Donland was tempted to loosen his neckerchief.

"Unbearably hot," Colonel Maitland stated.

"Aye," Donland agreed.

"You look undisturbed by the heat lieutenant," Maitland said to Morse.

"I've not moisture left in my body to sweat," Morse replied.

"Have you been ill?" Betty asked.

"Aye, dear lady, near a month. I was unconscious after a block came loose and split my skull. The surgeon gave me up but the good priest did not. His prayers and his tender care gave me a fighting chance."

"An accident?" Betty asked.

"It happened in battle. I was fourth aboard *Lion* and we were hammered by iron from starboard and larboard by two Frenchmen. A lot of good and decent lads perished that day. I was fortunate not to be counted among them."

"*Lion* is on station in Jamaica as I recall," Donland stated.

"Aye, it is my intention to rejoin her. Captain Cornwallis sent me home to recuperate."

"Home being Savannah?" Maitland inquired.

"Aye, this house. It belongs to my family."

"So we are your guests," Betty said with delight.

"Guests yes, but mine, no," Morse said with a hint of unease. "This house among others and certain parcels of land are collateral against loans."

"Oh, I'm dreadfully sorry to have infringed on your family's private affairs," Betty said and added, "please forgive me."

Morse smiled. "No need dear lady."

Donland noticed Sumerford's discomfort and the sudden dart of his eyes toward Morse at the mention of the collateral. No doubt Morse was beholding to Sumerford.

Two servants came in bearing platters.

Donland was glad of the interruption and delighted to see the food.

Conversation veered to Betty and her days in Charles Town. She made sparing comments as to the difficulty of finding dresses, the constant tension between loyalists and rebels when attending social functions. "So uncivilized," she said with a frown.

Sumerford said good-naturedly, "War is not civilized, at least this one is not."

Maitland snorted, "Nothing civilized about shooting men in the back!"

Sumerford half-frowned, "I do believe I've eaten enough for two. Cigars and brandy Colonel?"

"Brandy and the business at hand?" Maitland asked.

Sumerford did not answer but turned to Morse, "Join if you please Lieutenant."

Donland waited for the trio to leave before standing. He had no inkling as to Maitland's, *business at hand* but felt it was the reason for the dinner. He would, no doubt, be informed what his part would be in such business. Sumerford would disclose that part of the business at the appropriate time, his time.

David sat silent during the meal contending himself with the food. Donland watched him as he ate and wondered if there was enough food to fill the boy.

"David how have you been?" Betty asked.

David had just stuffed a large piece of meat into his mouth. He quickly chewed then swallowed.

"Well madam," he managed and took up his glass and drank deeply to wash the meat down.

She laughed and said, "You seem to not have neaten in a long while."

David's face reddened.

"Not since noon, biscuits and molasses," David said.

Donland sipped his wine and placed his glass back on the table. "I've eaten my fill to be sure." He turned to Betty, "A walk in the garden?" he asked.

"No dear, let us go to the parlor," she answered.

"It will be dreadfully hot," he said.

She smiled and said, "Perhaps, but I've something to say to you in private."

She turned away from him to David who sopped gravy with a piece of bread. "Eat as much as you like, there's plenty and there is pastry. The servant will bring it when you are ready."

David's eyes widened. "Thank you Miss Sumerford," he said.

Donland rose and extended his arm to Betty.

As she rose she said, "David, I've instructed the butler to prepare a place for you to sleep."

Donland was surprised and said, "I've not planned to stay. Your cousin did not indicate it was to be a lengthy visit, just dinner."

"That may have been his intention but not mine. You and David will stay," she said firmly.

"Oh that I could but not just this night but many. I've given orders to prepare to sail, and then there is Jackson to be seen too."

She caught the anxiety in his voice. "Something has happened to Mr. Jackson?"

"Aye, gravely wounded," Donland answered as he closed the door to the parlor.

"How?"

"He was ashore and went missing. We found him in an alley near death. He'd been knifed in the chest. The surgeon is not hopeful."

"Surely the man is wrong," she said.

"Your cousin swears by the man," he paused. "I've a man with him, a fellow who has proven himself an effective healer."

"Not a doctor or surgeon?" she asked.

He grinned, "No a witch-doctor so I'm told."

"Surely not!" She exclaimed."

"Aye, from all accounts. We'd lost Andrews were it not for him. But enough of that."

He drew her close and put his arms around her then kissed her. She buried her face in his neck and kissed it lightly.

Sumerford and Morse sat in the carriage waiting for Donland. His goodbye to Betty was lengthy. He had not wanted to go no more than she wanted to allow him to leave.

"Long night?" Sumerford teased.

Donland said nothing.

They rode in silence until well away from the house. Donland's mind as was his heart, was on Betty.

"Your other love calls you," Sumerford said. "It's time to be about our task and we've not much time to accomplish it. Is *Hornet* ready to sail?"

"Aye," Donland answered. He continued, "We've provisions and shot for a long voyage if necessary. My only shortage is in men and officers but there is naught I can do to remedy either."

Sumerford pursed his lips. "I prefer not to meddle in your command but my needs come before yours at the moment."

Donland was fully alert.

"Lieutenant Morse will be assisting me and therefore is temporarily assigned to *Hornet* and you may use him as you deem appropriate. As to men, I will borrow from the other ships in port to fill out your complement and there will be a few riflemen billeted aboard. I trust you will accept my intrusion as necessary."

Donland didn't like the intrusion. But, in his years of service, he knew such things were necessary. "I'm under your orders," he said without emotion.

"That too, that too," Sumerford said and continued. "Captain, I would not have made these decisions were it not of necessity. We will be bound for Jamaica and then onward as circumstance warrant. Our task is to ascertain the intentions of the French toward Savannah. I trust my informants and the information they have gleaned but my trust nor information seems sufficient for the governor."

"The riflemen, are they regular army or mercenaries?" Donland asked.

Sumerford answered, "Neither, they are backwoodsmen with tracking skills and skilled at remaining unobserved. Crack shots with those long rifles as well."

"Are they Colonel Maitland's scouts?"

Sumerford grinned and nodded.

Morse said nothing during the exchange. Donland judged by the man's silence that he was aware of the arrangements. And perhaps other unspoken arrangements.

"Will we be returning the Lieutenant to *Lion* on our return?" Donland asked.

"Yes and with my thanks," Sumerford answered.

Jackson lay as he had when Donland had last visited. Only Baako was present. He sat beside the bed holding a small wet piece of cloth.

"Has the doctor seen him today?" Donland asked.

"He not come again," Baako answered.

Jackson's chest was bare except for the blackish green salve covering the wound. A bowl of brown liquid sat on the table beside the bed. Baako took the cloth and dipped it into the bowl then pushed into Jackson's mouth.

"Is that medicine?" Donland asked.

"Food," Baako answered.

Donland watched his friend for several minutes. Baako withdrew the cloth and said, "Food make him strong."

Donland considered what Baako was doing and what the surgeon had said. Jackson had already lived longer than the surgeon anticipated. Either the surgeon, Baako or God was keeping Jackson alive. He didn't know whom to thank, and it mattered not as long as Jackson recovered.

The door opened. "Beg pardon sir, Mr. Ashcroft compliments, he asks that you come," David said with his hat tucked in the crook of his arm.

"Is there a problem Mr. Welles?

"Aye Sir, some rowdy men have come aboard. They're drunk and they say Mr. Sumerford sent them."

Donland smiled. "Aye, he did send them. I best come."

"Baako you are to remain here. Do not leave him. Donland pulled his purse and dug inside for coins. He handed them over to Baako, "Whatever you need or he needs, buy it. Do you understand?"

"Aye, aye Captain," Baako said accepting the coins.

It was all he could do for Jackson. *Hornet* would be sailing before nightfall and he did not know when or if he would return to see his friend.

Six men, two tall and thin, one of medium height and three short stubby men lounged on the foredeck. Packs and long rifles leaned against the gunnel. Each man sat sprawled with his back against the gunnel and either a jug or a bottle was in his hands.

"I told them to wait there for you," Ashcroft stated.

"Aye, that is well," Donland replied. "Make room for them in the forecastle hold and clear space in the main-hold for their dunnage. I'll have their rifles stored in the gunroom."

"Aye Captain, I'll put Endicott in charge. He is of the same ilk as these and better suited to deal with them."

"Very good. I'll have a word with them in a moment. I take it no one else has come aboard?"

Ashcroft's face showed puzzlement.

Donland clarified, "A Lieutenant Morse?"

"No sir, I've not seen him. Should we expect him?"

"Aye, he is on loan to us. I'll tell you more in my cabin after I've spoken to our guests."

Donland made his way forward. He was aware of the eyes on him; both those of his guests and those of the ship's company.

"I'm Captain Donland, Captain of the *Hornet*, who is in charge here?"

The men burst into laughter; none made to stand.

Donland waited. He determined it would do no good to be insistent with these men at this time.

The men settled then eyed him. He waited.

"Colonel Maitland sent us," the tall skinny man said.

"Aye, I know. I was expecting you, my apologies for not being present when you came aboard. Colonel Maitland spoke highly of you."

All six men straightened then stood.

The tall man said, "I'm Jonas Coles, these here fellows are Henry Johnson, Dawson Mcquirt, William Jenkins, Bill Miller and Shorty Jenkins."

"Good to meet you gentlemen. I'm having arrangements made for you to stow your belongs and rifles."

"Our rifles stay with us," Shorty Miller snarled.

Donland addressed Coles, "Mr. Coles you'll not need a rifle while we are at sea. They will be returned to you before we make landfall. No man aboard carries a weapon. The knives they carry are tools and your men may keep their knives. Pistols and rifles will be stored with the other armaments under lock and key. One of my men will come shortly and show you were you can sleep and store your belongings. Once you are settled in we'll discuss what we are to be about."

"I ain't giving no man my rifle," Shorty said defiantly.

Donland smiled giving himself time. It would serve no good purpose to antagonize these men. Shorty could be dealt with later and in a manner that would create less friction between the ship's company and the newcomers.

"Mr. Coles, for the moment the men can take their rifles below. We'll discuss it after you are settled in."

"Ain't taking . . ." That was all Shorty managed before Coles turned and knocked him to the deck.

"He'll be no more trouble Captain," Coles stated.

Donland extended his hand. "Pleased to have you aboard Mr. Coles."

"Thank you Captain, I'll deal with this lot, there'll be no trouble."

Sumerford came aboard at two bells in the afternoon. "In your cabin if you please Captain," he said as he moved toward the hatchway.

Donland followed him.

"When can you sail?" Sumerford asked.

Donland didn't hesitate, "Within the hour if required."

"Two will do," Sumerford said and plopped down in a chair. "Have you something cool to drink?"

"Aye," he answered and called, "Honest!"

"Aye Captain," Honest replied.

"Is he always lurking about?" Sumerford asked.

"Yes, he serves as coxs'n, his only duty is to look after my gig and be available to me as needed."

"A personal servant?"

Donland smiled, "No, much more than that, bodyguard, conscience and nursery-maid all in one."

"In other words a man you trust implicitly."

"Aye."

Honest came in bearing a brown jug and two glasses. "I fetched it straight from the bilge," he said and held out a glass for Sumerford then poured.

"Amazing!" Sumerford said. "You've not offered me any so cold before on our travels."

"You've not requested cold before, just wet," Honest replied.

"Your scouts have come aboard," Donland said changing the subject.

"Good, good," Sumerford said and added, "You'll have the men you need to fill out your crew before we sail. The governor made the arrangements."

Donland was not surprised the governor made the arrangements. Sumerford did not have the power to conscript men on his own.

Where are we bound?" he asked.

"Jamaica as I told you and from there as need arises. I'll not know until I reach Kingston. How many days will it take?"

"With favorable winds it should take no more than six days."

Sumerford's face grimaced. "Good winds and your best sail-handling?"

"Five and a half, no less," Donland said bluntly.

"Then let us be away as quickly as possible."

"As soon as the men the governor has arranged arrive, we will get underway. We have stores and fresh water for six weeks and will replenish what we use once we reach Jamaica. Is that sufficient for this voyage?"

"More than enough I should think."

A tapping at the cabin door interrupted them.

"Enter!" Donland called.

"Mr. Ashcroft's compliments Sir, the new hands are coming aboard," Aldridge reported.

"Thank you Mr. Aldridge, my compliments to Mr. Ashcroft, I shall come up shortly."

"Aye Sir," Aldridge said and turned to leave.

"I've taken the liberty to inform Mr. Dewitt of our destination when I came aboard. He will have charted the course. If your dunnage is aboard, we will make sail."

"I've what I need," Sumerford said.

"Then I will go up," Donland said with a faint smile.

Chapter Five

Ten men were waiting on the foredeck. Lieutenant Morse stood with his hands behind his back by the mast and Aldridge stood a pace behind him also with his hands clasped behind his back.

Someone must have whispered "Captain" because Morse turned.

Donland ignored those watching. "Mr. Ashcroft we will get underway. I will sort out that lot by the foremast in due time."

"Anchor is hove short," Ashcroft informed Donland and turned.

"Hands to capstan! Headsail sheets!" Ashcroft bellowed.

"Mr. Morse!" Donland yelled above the din of getting underway. "A word if you please!"

Morse hurried aft dodging men and cordage. Donland observed his movements and thought him awkward. He turned his attention to David.

"Mr. Welles take charge of those new men and lead them below to await me."

"Aye Captain," Welles answered.

Donland considered Morse before he spoke. He'd not had the opportunity to learn about the man or his abilities.

"Have you experience aboard a sloop?" He asked.

Morse answered, "A brig before *Lion*. Was only a midshipman but was aboard for a year."

"Very well, tend the foremast. Mr. Aldridge will assist you."

"Aye Captain," Morse answered.

"Main tops'l braces!" Ashcroft thundered.

Donland stood beside the wheel watching as *Hornet's* sails began to fill. The ratlines were alive with men swarming toward the yards. The former slaves were as agile and fearless sailors as any Donland had even observed.

Hornet gathered the wind and began to strain forward.

"Anchor's away!" Seaman Brewer cried out.

Asa Little spun the helm. "Steerage Captain!" he called.

"Mr. Ashcroft you have the deck, I will go below. At the next watch you and Mr. Morse will join me below," Donland said and started for the hatchway.

Sumerford was waiting.

"Five days," Sumerford said.

"And a half," Donland added.

"Or not at all," Sumerford mused.

"The card you've not played and the trick you hope to take?" Donland said as he made his way past Sumerford.

"You know me oh so well Isaac. The cards you see are not all the cards to be played. We shall run down to Jamaica but not to Kingston. Are you familiar with Lucea?"

"No, where is it?"

"West of Montego Bay, small bay, good anchorage."

Donland nodded. "I've not familiar with that part of the island. The tales I've heard are of pirates, renegades and slavers relegated to Kingston."

Sumerford explained, "Montego Bay is British, they produce huge quantities of sugar and are a major contributor to the slave trade. Order is maintained by a contingent of soldiers and there is a fort. But, the plantation owners more than the government rule inland and the western coast. So as you can imagine they indulge in enterprises that fill their coffers. Among them, are sellers of information who have ties to both the French and the Spanish. I plan to purchase all that is available. It will entail dealing with men who hold to no code, allegiance and have absolutely no integrity."

"And you know them well?" Donland asked.

"I've dealings with them before and came away with my life. One in particular I intend have the better of."

"That one is the one who sold your name to those pirates who held the Portuguese prince?"

"As your Mr. Jackson would say, aye!"

"When we arrive you will be going ashore and inland?" Donland asked.

"Of necessity, yes. That is why I have engaged the scouts. Should the meeting not go to my advantage I shall need to be rescued."

"Are you not afraid for your life?"

Sumerford smiled broadly. "No, I'm worth too much alive to him. The French and the Spanish will pay handsomely to have conversations with me."

"If they are so willing to make such an offer, perhaps I should entertain an offer," Donland mused.

Redness showed in Sumerford's face, "Watch your tongue for I may offer you instead."

A knock at the door drew Donland's attention from the log entry. "Enter!" he called.

Ashcroft and Morse entered; each with their hats tucked in the crooks of their elbows.

"Gentlemen please take a seat," Donland began.

They sat.

"A glass of wine?" Donland asked.

Ashcroft looked to Morse and Morse to Ashcroft. It was Morse who answered, "Thank you kindly Captain, but no as I'm to return to the deck."

"I also," Ashcroft said.

"Gentlemen I've asked you below because I have neglected my duty. I don't know which of you is senior. Mr. Ashcroft's commission is dated August 1777 I believe."

"Aye sir," Ashcroft confirmed.

Morse half-grinned and said, "Mine is July that same year."

Donland could not keep himself from frowning. He instantly replaced it with blankness. "For this voyage Mr. Morse you will serve as acting first and Mr. Ashcroft as second. Good day gentleman, return to your duties."

"Aye Captain," Morse said without enthusiasm.

Ashcroft remained blank. "Aye, Captain," he managed before rising.

"Beg pardon Captain, Mr. Morse's compliments we've sighted Cape Florida," Aldridge announced.

"Thank you Mr. Aldridge. My compliments to Mr. Morse, maintain heading until the noon sighting."

"Aye Captain," Aldridge answered.

Donland turned his attention back to the log before him. He had just noted the amount of water in the bilge and his concern that there was a larger leak than had thus been noted. He would have to inspect the hull before the day was done. It annoyed him that Morse should have found the leak. Jackson would have found it and repaired it. He missed the man and his ways.

Overhead was a layer of thin cloud diffusing the sun. Aldridge and David were waiting when Donland came on deck. *Hornet* had a full press of canvas and was heeled to larboard.

"I make it north twenty-four and fourteen by west eighty-two and two," Dewitt said.

Donland took the sextant from Aldridge, checked the settings and brought it to his eye. "Aye, enter it Mr. Welles, he said.

"Aye Captain," David replied.

Donland noticed Sumerford nestled on the bowsprit reading a book. He wondered what the man might be reading but chose not to investigate. Perhaps over supper he would ask.

"Mr. Morse I shall go below," Donland said and started for the hatchway. As an afterthought he said, "If you please, join me in the main hold and bring a lantern. We shall inspect the hull."

Morse's face showed a hint of surprise but answered, "Aye Captain."

On his way below he called to Honest John to fetch a lantern and to follow him.

With the use of the lantern held by Honest, Donland began to examine the ribs. He felt certain one of them was the source of the leak. The planking was no doubt loosened by one of *Concorde's* balls. All he found was the usual dampness but not even a trickle of water. The leak was going to require greater effort to locate.

Morse clattered down the ladder.

"Join us if you please Mr. Morse, more light will not come amiss," Donland said as he continued inspecting a rib.

With both lanterns the hold was considerably brighter. So much so that Donland could see the bilge was almost full and sloshing onto the floorboards.

Morse was also aware of the amount of water. "I'll have it pumped when we finish," he said.

"When was it last pumped?" Donland asked.

"Four bells sir," Morse answered.

"Too much water, too fast or else the men did a poor work of it," Donland said.

"Mr. Welles saw to the pumping," Morse said uncomfortably.

Donland did not reply. In His mind, he was certain David would have had the well pumped as dry as possible. It only confirmed his fear, there was serious leakage. Heeled as *Hornet* was, the leak had to be larboard.

The three of them finished inspecting the hold and found no leak.

"Honest go onto the deck and fetch us three men," Donland ordered.

"Aye Captain," Honest replied.

"Mr. Morse I fear our problem may be at the waterline on the bow. We'll have the sail-locker emptied and the forward hold emptied then have another go at it. Set the men to it when they come down.

"Aye Captain," Morse replied.

Less than an hour later Morse reported to Donland, "You were correct captain. The leak was behind one of the bow ribs. I've men working to plug it from the inside. When we next tack I'll send a man over the side to add oakum and tar."

"Very well Mr. Morse. See to it if you please," Donland said.

He saw no need to observe the leak himself. Morse would have no doubt that the leak should have been discovered before now and stopped. It was the first lieutenant's responsibility. He sighed heavily after Morse left, *Jackson would have seen to it!*

Chapter Six

"Deck there! Sail on the larboard beam!"

Hornet was nearing Jamaica and sightings of other ships were to be expected.

"Frigate!" The lookout called down minutes later.

Donland hurried and clamped his hat on his head.

"Where away?" he called as he came through the hatch.

"To larboard, aft quarter Captain!" the lookout called down.

"Bearing away from us," Morse said.

"Aye," Donland agreed as he watched her through the glass. "*Concorde* as I live and breathe."

"Frenchman Sir?" Morse asked.

"Aye, and I'd not want to tangle with her without assistance. The *Ariadne* has been trying to run her to ground and either sink or capture her."

"She must have escaped Captain Pringle," Morse mused.

"Either that or the Frenchman got the better of the engagement," Donland answered. "No matter, she is going away from us."

"Wonder we'd not seen her sooner?" Morse asked.

Donland had the same thought. He put the glass to his eye again and studied *Concorde*. All her sails were set; no change in heading.

"She must have been laying-to," Donland said as much to himself as to Morse. He studied her a moment longer. "My guess is she saw our topsails and got underway."

Two hours after the sun broke over the horizon Donland was called. The sky was empty of cloud and the wind held steady.

"Montego Bay." Dewitt said.

"Thank you Mr. Dewitt. Maintain this heading let us stay parallel to the coast."

Donland studied the purple smudge through the telescope. There was not much to see at that distance.

"Mr. Morse send another man up with a glass. Two sets of eyes would not come amiss. I want to know the instant any sail is sighted. I fear this coast may not be to our liking."

"Aye Sir," Morse replied.

"Little aloft with you and take a glass," Morse ordered.

Asa Little looked befuddled. He looked from Dewitt to Donland.

"Belay Mr. Morse, Little has the wheel," Donland said with irritation.

"Honest up with you," Donland ordered.

"Beg pardon Captain," Morse managed as he realized his mistake. "I had meant to send Miller and got the name wrong."

"No matter," Donland said.

Donland was not aware of Sumerford's approach. He turned when Sumerford spoke, "Captain Donland I've a matter to discuss. In your cabin, if you please?"

"Wine Mathias?" Donland asked.

49

"It would not come amiss," Sumerford said.

Donland opened the locker and brought out two glasses from the rack and a bottle of wine. He poured and asked, "You are concerned about Lieutenant Morse?"

"Yes, I, like you have noticed he has moments of confusion."

Donland nodded but said nothing. He sipped his glass.

Sumerford held the glass but did not drink. "I would hazard to say that his being knocked about is still causing him some difficulty."

"I think so," Donland said. "I've a bit of a dilemma."

Sumerford took the bit between his teeth. "To continue to allow him to be your first officer or not?"

"Aye, because if we are engaged I'd not know if I could trust his judgement."

It was Sumerford's turn to nod. "Let us hope that we do not become engaged."

A hail interrupted them. "Three sail to starboard two points!" Honest called down.

"I must go up Mathias, I'll not make any change as yet."

Sumerford said, "I would prefer not at all."

Donland did not answer. *Hornet* was his first concern, Sumerford's need or even Morse's, for that matter, would not enter into his decision.

Donland turned away from the door. It needed to be said, "Mathias this vessel is under your orders. Even so, those aboard are under my command. I accepted Mr. Morse with misgivings; his health is questionable, as is his judgement. If I deem him to be a hazard to *Hornet,* I will not hesitate to replace him. At this point in time I will continue with him as first lieutenant. Tread lightly my friend and value my judgment."

It was Sumerford's turn not to answer.

Donland opened the door and left Sumerford to consider his words.

The ships sighted consisted of two fishermen and an armed brig flying no colors. The brig carried eight cannon, four to each side. To Donland's eye she was poorly maintained.

"Appears to be a pirate armed with long nines," Morse observed.

"Aye," Ashcroft agreed.

"She's not changed her tack even having seen us," Morse said.

Donland heard both but chose not to answer. His concern was on the coastline. He was not on this coast to take a prize; such would only complicate the task.

"Gentlemen unless there is a threat we will not engage. The chart shows a small cove, Mosquito Cove, three miles east of Lucea, which is where Mr. Sumerford will be conducting business. We shall set him ashore and he will go overland with the men he has brought aboard. Our task thus far is transport and support. If Mr. Sumerford is successful with his business we will return at once to Savannah. I am telling you this so you understand why we will not engage unless threatened. Our task is one requiring speed and diligence."

"Captain will we send men ashore?" Ashcroft asked.

"No, and ask no more, tend to your duty and we shall be away before nightfall," Donland said with finality.

"I'll be no more than two hours. Your ship's presence would have been announced by now so the man I seek will be expecting a visit but not one from me. One of my men will return to where the boat landed if the meeting sours. You will sail for Savannah for by the time he comes to you I will be beyond rescue."

Donland understood Sumerford's meaning. Betty would not be forgiving if he returned without her cousin.

Sumerford and his men departed in the launch crewed by eight men. Lieutenant Morse commanded the launch and accompanied Sumerford inland. The launch would remain on the beach until either Sumerford showed or one of his men.

As *Hornet* waited, Donland kept the anchor hove short and all men at their stations. He had taken the added measure of having two guns loaded with shot and two guns loaded with grape to guard against an attack for the shore. The other battery was manned and loaded with shot if by chance the brig should appear.

The sky showed signs of squalls within hours. The sun seemed unmercifully hot. Sweat beaded on Donland's face and his back was wet with sweat under his coat. As *Hornet* rocked gently on the waves, he was alert to all movement and sound.

He was not surprised to hear the faint *crack crack crack* of rifles an hour after Sumerford's leaving.

"Mr. Ashcroft man the capstan," Donland ordered.

He then lifted a glass to his eye and scanned the beach. There was no movement. The crew of the launch stood ready to depart. They too had heard the rifle shots and had drawn pistols. To his eye, all was in readiness to make a hurried departure whether or not Sumerford appeared.

Several more shots were heard, closer this time.

"Mr. Ashcroft send men aloft!" Donland shouted.

"Mr. Dewitt stand by the wheel! Helmsman at the ready!"

He saw them as they streamed from the jungle. With the glass to his eye, he spotted Sumerford in the mix. The firing of muskets became mixed with the crack of rifle shots. No doubt Sumerford was being pursued. Men began pouring into the launch, others turned and fired.

"Mr. Aldridge fire a shot on my command, hold the grape!" Donland commanded.

He did not wait to hear Aldridge reply.

The launch was away.

"Raise our hook! Make sail Mr. Ashcroft!"

"Aye Captain!" Ashcroft answered.

"Mr. Welles we will tow the launch, make it fast!"

"Aye Captain!" Welles answered and called men to him.

Donland lifted the glass to his eye. At the edge of the beach was a cluster of men. "Tree line Mr. Aldridge! Fire one gun when you bear!" Donland shouted.

"Aye Captain!" Aldridge acknowledged.

No more than ten seconds passed before the gun banged.

Donland gauged the shot and saw it splinter a treetop to the left of the cluster men. They hurried into the brush.

The launch was a third of the way to *Hornet*. Donland turned to the cove entrance. He was pleased to see that it was empty.

The crew of the launch was putting their backs into the rowing.

"Steerage Captain!" Dewitt called.

The launch bumped alongside. In seconds the men were pouring over the side. David shouted down to the men still in the launch to make it fast for towing.

Sumerford came over the side followed by Morse. Donland counted the men. They were all present plus one. Donland surmised that capturing the man had been Sumerford's true objective.

The scouts came aboard celebrating, backslapping and rollicking.

"Mr. Morse get those men below!" Donland bellowed.

"Aye Captain!" Morse answered and the smile on his face disappeared.

Sumerford, smiling came across to Donland. "No need to be harsh," he said.

Donland ignored him.

He turned to Dewitt, "Take us out Mr. Dewitt. Steer West by southwest, we'll round the island and set a course for the Windwards."

"Aye Captain," Dewitt replied.

"Mr. Ashcroft set all sail once we clear the cove," Donland ordered.

Donland called to Bill up on the mast, "What of the brig?"

"Steering south by southeast!" Bill called down.

"Mr. Aldridge secure the guns!"

"Aye Captain!" Aldridge answered.

"Captain I'd like a word with you," Sumerford said.

Donland spoke his mind. "Very well in my cabin. But, I'd say it is unnecessary for I see you achieved your objective and now we can continue our task. There is no need for explanations."

Hornet responded to the change of tack and to the prevailing winds. Donland's mind wasn't on the ship handling. Sumerford followed him below. They did not speak until the door was closed.

"I understand your anger for not telling you what I was about," Sumerford began. "But it was necessary for you'd not been agreeable to my methods. The man had to be taken by any means possible and I knew that it would require considerable force. I sought to spare you and your men from harm."

"Aye, you did that," Donland said then asked, "What was Lieutenant Morse's role in this?"

"He is a good friend to the man we brought aboard. I knew that his appearance would smooth the path, so to speak."

"And what did it cost Mr. Morse to go along with you and betray his friend?"

Sumerford did not answer but instead drew his case and extracted one of his foul-smelling cigars. He lit, and it and blew a plume of blue smoke.

"Doesn't concern me?" Donland asked.

"No it doesn't," Sumerford answered. "But, I will tell you this, he repaid a debt."

"And you are keen on collecting debts," Donland asserted.

"When it suits my purposes," Sumerford answered

A knock at the door ended the discussion.

"Enter!" Donland barked.

"Beg pardon captain, Mr. Morse's compliments, the brig has changed course," David reported.

"Thank you Mr. Welles. What of the new course?"

"Due east sir."

The course change disturbed Donland. He knew it would come but thought it would be later.

"My compliments to Mr. Morse and he is to keep me advised."

"Aye Captain," David replied and went out.

"Trouble?" Sumerford asked.

"That depends on what you can tell me about her ownership," Donland said.

Sumerford grinned. "You are beginning to piece it together.

"Aye, dimly," Donland answered.

"The man below is accountable to the French and to the English. He supplies both with information about the other. The brig is his, and he uses it as a courier. She is well armed and perhaps more than a match for you. Mr. Morse can tell you more about her qualities as he has been aboard her on more than one occasion."

Donland was not surprised at the revelation. Morse should have been hung as a traitor but was not because of his involvement with Sumerford. No doubt the lieutenant was in Sumerford's debt and acted accordingly. The man was a pawn.

"I will inquire of Mr. Morse but before I do, will he be truthful?"

Again Sumerford grinned. "He will and happily. His life depends on whether or not you decide to engage the brig."

"And if I do?"

"The brig will not be easily subdued and in the heat of the battle many lives will be lost and his among them. The man is not a fool, and he knows me well. I would strike him down should he practice deceit and he knows it."

"So an enemy at his front and an enemy at his back will keep him honest?"

"That it will do," Sumerford replied and blew more smoke.

Donland picked up the pitcher of water from the sideboard and poured. He thought as he drank. He, like Morse, was a pawn. *Hornet* just a vehicle for Sumerford's schemes. He decided to know more before circumstances unfolded and he was forced to react with limited knowledge.

"I have been tasked by you to Jamaica," Donland began, "and then onward to the Windward Islands. The passage is to be swift and we are to avoid entanglements with other ships. Is that still what we are about?"

"Yes," Sumerford answered.

"And yon brig intends to shadow us and wait for an opportunity to take us?"

"I would say that is his intention. But, he'd not know we have Swail aboard."

Sumerford had just given up the last piece of the puzzle. "He is your insurance against attack? You have him for your own purposes and his friends dare not interfere."

Sumerford blew more smoke.

Donland's neck was hot with anger. He shook his head and picked up his hat. "I need some air," he said and went out.

The plan began to form in Donland's mind as he made his way to the helm. He took the strongest telescope and scanned the sea. The brig was following, pacing *Hornet*. He stepped close to Dewitt, "We will go about Mr. Dewitt and I will have words with her captain."

"Aye captain," Dewitt agreed.

Donland could tell by the gleam in Dewitt's eyes and the half-smile that the man understood it would not be a social visit. No not by half it would not.

He called to David, "Mr. Welles come over if you please, I have a message."

The boy came over.

Prepare *'have Swail aboard'*. The name is Swail, do you understand?"

"Aye Captain, have Swail aboard, s-w-a-i-l," David replied.

"Good, you will hoist it when I command."

"Aye Captain," the youngster answered.

Donland called to Ashcroft, "Make ready to go about Mr. Ashcroft!"

"Aye Captain," Ashcroft answered.

"Hands aloft! Prepare to wear ship!"

Aldridge was at the ready, "Lee braces there! Hands wear ship!"

Donland eyed the brig. She had made no changes in sail. Overhead came the squeal of blocks and tackle.

"Tops'l sheets!" Aldridge shouted.

The brig's captain had to be aware that *Hornet* was wearing ship. Several seconds passed as *Hornet* entered her turn before he saw the movement of the brig's sails. She was reducing sail.

The brig maintained steerage. Surprisingly, Sumerford remained below as *Hornet* came about. Donland assumed he was having a conversation with Swail and Morse. That was good, he'd have no interference. It was time to execute his plan.

Still watching the brig he called, "Honest fetch Bill and his mates. I've a task for them."

"Aye," Honest replied and set off.

"Mr. Ashcroft, have the launch prepared to lower if you please," Donland called.

They were nearing rowing distance for the launch. He judged from the activity aboard the brig that they were preparing for either flight or fight. "Mr. Welles, the signal if you please," he called to the boy.

"Mr. Ashcroft have the launch put over," Donland called. Those who had just recovered the launch from Sumerford's foray ashore would not be thanking him for the task of launching it again.

Bill stepped forward followed by twelve of the former slaves. Donland said, "Bill, you and your mates will man the launch. Every man will need a knife. There may be need of some quick cutting, be prepared for a fight."

Bill smiled broadly, "Aye Captain we do cutting good."

Donland gave his attention to the brig. Preparations had ceased, and they seemed to be waiting. No doubt the captain had watched the lowering of the launch. He was expecting a visit from Swail.

"Mr. Welles, my compliments to Mr. Sumerford and Mr. Morse, have them to come on deck and bring Mr. Swail along."

"Aye Captain," David answered.

Donland waited, he measured distance and time before speaking. "Mr. Dewitt once we gain the brig's deck lay *Hornet* alongside."

He turned to Ashcroft. "Arm our company, once *Hornet* is alongside you are to make fast with grapples and send them across."

"Aye Captain," Ashcroft answered. His face showed nothing.

"It is my intention to take her as a prize," Donland added for clarity.

Sumerford and the two others came on deck. Sumerford immediately went to Donland. "What do you intend?" he asked.

"I'll not be shadowed by the likes of that," he said and continued, "with the armament you have indicated she is a threat and one that has to be nullified. My intention is to board her and seize her with or without your cooperation but I prefer with it. As to Mr. Swail, he is yours to do as you deem fit, I'll not interfere."

Sumerford looked toward the brig and then back at Donland. "The brig is of no concern if you can manage without damage to this vessel and her crew."

"Aye, that is also my intention. We will go aboard along with Mr. Swail. They'll suspect nothing if he and a boat full of slaves goes across to her."

Sumerford nodded. "Subterfuge, I understand well."

"Say nothing to Swail, let him think we are returning him," Donland said.

Swail seemed to be full of himself as the launch came near to the brig. The beefy man even smiled. He was wise enough not to say anything. The launch bumped alongside the brig, Swail was the first up and out. Donland followed close behind and was ready to deal with the man should he raise alarm.

A rail-thin short man met them. The beard and the cruelty in the man's eye kept him from being mistaken for a boy.

"Mr. Swail, good to see you I'd not expected you to have managed a king's ship for transport," the brig captain said.

"Treachery, Tompkins, comes in all forms," Swail said without raising his voice.

Confusion registered on Tompkins' face.

Donland stepped forward, "Commander Donland of *Hornet*," he said while drawing his sword.

Alarm replaced the confusion on Tompkins' face as Bill and his mates came over the railing and spread out. Morse, for some reason, remained in the launch.

"What is this?" Tompkins demanded.

"I require the use of this vessel Mr. Tompkins. I understand Mr. Swail owns it, and therefore you will offer no resistance. And if you should, your life will be forfeit," Donland said firmly.

The first grapple went across and Tompkins turned. As the next one landed and he said, "Treachery is the right word."

Donland asked, "Well?"

Tompkins asked, "Mr. Swail have you orders?"

Men began leaping across from *Hornet* with raised muskets and pistols.

"Do as he says," Swail managed with bitterness in his voice.

Ashcroft came to Donland's side and Donland turned to him, "Lower the brig's boats and put her crew into them. We're no more than a few miles from shore and they can manage the pull."

"Aye captain," Ashcroft replied and asked, "what of the brig?"

"She'll need a captain and a fit crew. I would think Bill and his mates sufficient and you are more than capable for command," Donland answered.

"Thank you Captain, it would be my pleasure," Ashcroft replied.

"Mr. Sumerford do you have further use of Mr. Swail?" Donland asked.

"Yes he and I have other matters. He will remain with us," Sumerford answered.

"Very well then. He will be in your charge. You may attend to him in my cabin."

"That will be suitable," Sumerford replied and added, with your permission we shall go across."

Seeing Honest Donland called, "Honest my compliments to Mr. Morse, have him come to me."

Donland had wondered where the man had gotten. It was in his mind to put him in command of the brig. But, he had not come aboard from the launch and that raised caution in his mind. Sumerford's phrase of, *an enemy to the front and an enemy to the back* came to mind. He did not trust Morse and it would be better to keep him close.

"We'll not call at Kingston," Sumerford stated.

"Aye, I agree, *Lion's* captain would have questions," Donland said.

"On to the east and with the brig in tow?" Sumerford asked.

"Aye," Donland answered and asked, "Swail had no information concerning French intentions?"

"No more than we already know. The French are under pressure from the colonials to attack either New Orleans or Savannah. They believe once they secure either then we will be beaten and have to surrender the colonies," Sumerford answered.

"We've no choice then but to go in search of the French fleet," Donland said.

"No choice," Sumerford said half-heartily. He asked, "How long to Martinique?"

Donland did not hesitate, "Four days with good wind to Guadeloupe, six to Martinique." Then he asked the question that was plaguing him, "Any chance the French have already sailed?"

Sumerford's face showed nothing. "I would say not. Swail would have given it up to stay on his plantation."

"So you tried to bargain with him?"

"Yes, but he had nothing to bargain with," Sumerford admitted.

Chapter Seven

Donland had debated sinking the brig but had also considered that she may be useful. The long nines she carried allowed for far greater reach than *Hornet's* armament. Being just over half the length of *Hornet* she could be formidable in the right hands. His concern was manpower. Eighteen men could manage a short voyage but her sail requirements necessitated double that for anything other than island trading. He had set forty-two afloat of her original crew. None were willing to join *Hornet's* company and pressing any of them would be a risk he was not willing to undertake.

He determined that the brig even lightly manned would be an asset. French or Spanish frigates would consider the odds before taking on the pair. They'd not know the brig had less than a full company aboard until they came close. If it came to it, he could scuttle her at any time. Ashcroft would be sore disappointed at losing his command.

Sumerford's scouts managed to cause trouble. Donland ordered their spirits confiscated but they'd found other sources.

They were an unruly bunch and two were confined in the hold, the others he put to pumping the bilge once every watch. Three others he sent aboard the brig *Diana*.

Ashcroft was managing with the men he had but the *Diana* was a poor sailor. Donland reluctantly sent eight more hands across when he sent the scouts. The additional hands would have no rest.

Of Morse, Donland was still trying to sort the man out. He seemed capable on one hand and a buffoon on the other. Mr. Aldridge had to remind him of several basic tasks, those any midshipman would do automatically. Donland feared the man's mind was failing. Being at sea did not bring improvement. Dewitt had agreed to be on deck as much as possible when it was not his watch. Donland did the same.

Dawn of the third day brought the hail Donland had feared. "Deck there! Sail to the north!"

The morning sun had shone briefly off of topsails. Two hours passed without another sighting. He argued the decision in his mind and finally decided.

"We will lie-to Mr. Morse," Donland said with reluctance.

"Hands aloft!" Morse shouted. "Reef all sails!"

There were many possibilities but only one that nagged Donland's mind. The more he thought about, the more absurd it seemed yet he could not shake it. He dared not voice the possibility. Better, he thought, to allow his suspicion to play out. *Concorde* was a fast sailor for a frigate and if she were stalking *Hornet,* he would soon know. He reasoned the French captain would have discovered that Sumerford and Swail were aboard. They and *Hornet* would be a prize worth taking. The man was a fox to all accounts and if his suspicion were correct the Frenchman was bidding his time to take *Hornet* with the least risk to his ship. Better to force the Frenchman's hand than be taken unaware.

Dewitt came on deck. "Beg pardon Captain, are we laying-to?"

"Aye, for a time," Donland answered.

Bill was aboard the *Diana* so Donland called to Honest, "Aloft with you and take a strong glass. A sail was reported to the north and I fear our shadow has not left us."

"Aye Captain!" Honest said and removed his shoes before starting for the shrouds.

"Beg pardon captain, message from *Diana*," Aldridge said.

Donland had seen the flags. "Send continue on course," he said before Aldridge stated the message.

He could wait for *Diana* to close the distance but could not wait for her to reach *Hornet*. If the sail was indeed *Concorde*, *Hornet* would have to sail before the wind and there would be no time to save those aboard the brig.

"What of the wind Mr. Dewitt?" Donland asked.

"Same as yesterday and will be the same tomorrow, northeast to southeast, steady and about fifteen knots. Might grow to twenty by the dogwatch. Closer in toward the Windwards there'll be more squalls."

Hornet would be hard pressed to gain any distance and *Diana* had no chance at all. She was a good deal slower than *Hornet* with her small prize crew. The decision was a hard one, abandon *Diana* or wait for her to come up to *Hornet*. The French captain would by now have recognized that *Diana* had only a prize crew aboard and be of little threat to his ship.

"Deck there!" Honest called down, "*Concorde!*"

Donland's fear was voiced in that one word but what to do now. Continue to wait, run or turn and fight?

Diana had a full set of sail aloft but she was ungainly, yawing before the wind. She would be in range of *Concorde's* bow chasers within an hour. Donland decided to wait, it was a foolish wishful choice. There was an outside chance the French captain would bide his time in hopes of taking two prizes instead of a small one.

Donland lifted the glass *Concorde's* topsails were just becoming visible. Diana continued onward at her slow pace. He gauged the wind and the sea while he waited. Lifting the glass again to his eye he found the Frenchman. Her bow crest and heel of the hull told him she could not gain another knot. She was flying before the wind as if the devil himself were chasing her.

"Why are you so eager?" Donland asked aloud.

"Sir?" David asked.

Donland lowered the glass and turned to the boy, "Thinking aloud, pay it no mind."

"Deck there!" Honest shouted down. "Second sail!"

"Where away?" Donland called.

"Wake of *Conconde* Captain!"

Donland again lifted the glass but saw nothing. The second ship must just be coming over the horizon and from the maintop perch, Honest was able to see her.

"Is she *Ariadne?*" Donland called up.

Seconds passed before Honest called, "No!"

A half-minute later Honest called, "I can't make her out Captain!"

Donland checked *Diana*; she was still surging forward. He said to David, "Send up 'make more sail,' if you please Mr. Welles."

"Aye Captain," David answered.

The signal would do no good for Ashcroft was doing all he could with what it had. But, the French captain would read the signal and hopefully assume the sloop before him would continue to wait for the brig.

"Mr. Morse prepare to make sail, call all hands," Donland commanded.

"Aye Captain," Morse answered.

Donland lifted the glass again to study *Concorde*. She was unchanged.

Men were hurrying to their stations and climbing the shrouds to lose the sails when ordered. The French captain would be watching and would anticipate that *Hornet* would flee and leave the brig to his bidding.

Donland called up to Honest, "What of the second sail?"

"Third rate!" Honest called down.

The words startled Donland. He was expecting the *Ariadne*.

"Repeat!" Donland called up.

"Third rate, Captain! I've no doubt!"

"Mr. Morse go aloft if you please and identify that ship," Donland ordered.

"Aye captain," Morse answered and took the telescope Donland held out to him.

Morse went no further than midway of the shrouds. He focused and without removing the glass from his eye called; "It's the *Lion*!"

Donland had thought the same when Honest had announced the newcomer was a third-rate.

"Mr. Morse we will go about," Donland said.

In the next breath he ordered, "Mr. Welles signal *Diana* to go about, enemy in sight. Once acknowledged send up, 'tack to her starboard bow'."

"Aye Captain," David answered.

"Loose top gal'ent's stays'ls and royals," Morse bellowed.

As soon as they were sheeted home *Hornet* began slipping through the water with the ease of a knife.

Donland waited for *Hornet* to gain her pace then ordered, "Go about Mr. Morse."

The hands began to haul the braces around.

"Tacks and sheets!" Morse shouted

"Mainsail haul!"

Hornet was like a racehorse charging into the turn. The helmsman held her in check as she turned.

Donland turned and checked *Diana*, she was beginning her turn. She would be slow. No matter, the Frenchman would have to make a decision to either fight or run. With *Lion* bearing down, any delay could be deadly.

"Deck there!" Honest cried out, his voice almost lost in the wind.

"Sail bearing down from westward!"

Donland pulled the glass from the rack that he had given Morse. There was no mistaking *Ariadne*. Captain Cornwallis must have sent her wide to scout for *Conconde*. She had the wind up her coattails and was surging forward to intercept. Now it was up to *Hornet* to be a stopper in a bottle.

"What do you intend?" Sumerford asked.

Donland had been unaware of Sumerford's presence. The man had chosen to be an observer until now.

"Only to slow yon frigate that *Lion* may render her ineffective," he said without taking his eye from *Ariadne*.

"Is that advisable?" Sumerford asked.

"Aye, it is. I believe her intentions were to have two birds in hand and none in the bush. On her present tack she can rake *Diana* and *Hornet* as she passes. Her captain is no fool, with a third-rate bearing down he'll choose to turn away from us. He'll not chance our damaging his sail and rigging leaving him crippled to face a larger foe."

Donland called to David, "Mr. Welles send to *Diana* to engage more closely!"

Ashcroft would know to keep his distance and to fire at full elevation in hopes of damaging *Concorde's* rigging. That is what *Hornet* would intend as well.

Dewitt said behind Donland, "She's tacking!"

"Aye as expected," Donland answered.

"Mr. Dewitt alter course and keep us running ahead of her."

Donland checked *Diana*, Ashcroft was reading his mind and was altering course to be an obstacle in the frigate's path. It was dangerous but necessary. *Lion* had no hope of gaining on the frigate without *Hornet* and *Diana* providing interference.

Ariadne was coming up fast. *Lion* had altered her course. *Concorde* may well escape if she could evade damage to her sails.

Donland did not see *Concorde's* gun ports open. She fired a slow roll of starboard guns at *Diana*. Only one ball plucked at the small ship's rigging. Immediately *Diana* began falling off as her fore-course sails went slack and began to flap. It was now up to *Hornet* and she was at extreme range for her small guns.

"Mr. Morse I'll see to the guns. Get us closer!" Donland said as he left the quarterdeck.

"Larboard gun crews to me!" he shouted.

Men scrambled to their guns.

"Unlash the guns and load! Double charges and full elevation!" he said as he moved from gun to gun.

Looking up, he gauged the distance to *Concorde*, she was slightly ahead. *Hornet's* guns were no match for her but they could wound and that was all he sought.

So intent was he with the guns that he did not see *Concorde's* guns run out again. It was only when the first of three balls tore into the rigging that he knew she had fired. Lines twanged as they parted. He heard the *poof, poof* of the balls as they tore through the sails.

"Ready!" the first gun captain called.

Donland jumped to the gun. "Wedge it round left!"

"More!" he shouted.

The crew obeyed. He held the slow match, *Hornet* plunged into a wave and lifted her bow. He tugged the lanyard, and the gun boomed and rocked back.

"Ready!" the captain of the next gun shouted.

"Up!" Donland ordered.

He sighted and fired the gun.

"Ready!" the next captain called.

A shout rose from the deck, and then another and the whole of the ship began to cheer. Donland sighted the next gun and to his amazement saw the mizzenmast of *Concorde* come crashing down.

He stepped back in relief.

"Mr. Dewitt hard over to starboard," Donland shouted.

"Aye Captain!" Dewitt answered. Immediately *Hornet* heeled.

A thunderous roar forward shook *Hornet* as two heavy balls from *Concorde* struck. Splinters from the railing and planking shot out like daggers. Men went down withering in puddles of their own blood. Wails of pain filled the air. Few noticed the many splashes of iron balls less than a cable off *Hornet's* hull.

Donland picked himself up off the deck. There was no more cheering.

"Secure the guns Dawkins," Donland ordered as he made his way forward.

Men were down; Donland counted ten. "See to the wounded!" He shouted to two seamen staring at the carnage.

Reaching the bow, he leaned out over the side while holding to a line. The damage was above the waterline but no doubt water would be pouring in where seams had opened.

"You men with me!" he called to three men trying to clear away an upended gun.

A roar of cannon caused him to look toward the sound. *Lion* had fired a broadside. She was barely within her range for any ball to strike the injured *Concorde*. But more than one ball had found the mark. The beautiful frigate was hard hit. Her sails were in tatters and rigging hung like confetti.

"Let us see to our needs," he said to the three men.

The men followed Donland down the hatchway. To their horror water was pouring in.

"Cut down the hammocks!" Donland ordered. "Stuff those seams! Hurry, we've no time."

He turned to the hatchway. More men were needed to stem the rushing water. The damage above deck could wait; the water would not.

Honest met him at the hatchway. "Gather ten men and get them below. We've got to stop the water."

"Aye Captain," Honest answered.

Donland continued to the helm. "Mr. Dewitt get the way off the ship. We've water rushing in."

"Mr. Morse man the pumps, every man jack able is to take a turn. Keep em' fresh."

"Aye Captain!" Morse answered weakly.

"What can I do?" Sumerford asked.

"Take a hand at the pump if you please. That's our real danger."

Donland's next concern was the wounded. He went from man to man checking the wounded. Three were dead and two others would soon be. It was a heavy price to pay just to alter a ship's direction. He turned as a cheer went up.

Ariadne was alongside *Concorde*. The French flag had come down. What *Hornet* had begun, *Lion* had added weight and now Pringle of *Ariadne* had his revenge.

"Signal from *Lion*, captain," David said. "They ask if we need assistance."

Donland thought for a moment then said, "Request a surgeon and a carpenter."

"Aye Captain," David answered.

As an afterthought Donland asked, "What of *Diana?*"

"There sir," David answered and pointed to larboard. She lay more than a mile away with her sails furled. No doubt she too was licking her wounds.

"Mr. Welles, send to *Diana*, 'do you require assistance?'"

Dawkins came from below and asked, "Beg pardon Captain, can you come below?"

"What's the trouble Dawkins?"

"The pumps sir, they're not keeping up."

Donland surveyed the deck, "Is Mr. Morse below supervising?"

"He's not Captain, we've not seen him."

Anger burned in Donland but he smothered it. "I'll come."

The seams they had managed to staunch earlier in the voyage had opened and there were others from the shot spewing water.

Donland took in the damage and said, "I've sent for *Lion's* carpenter he should be able to deal with these seams. Let me hold the lantern."

Asa Little passed the lantern to Donland. He began to examine the planking just below the decking. Daylight was showing through where planking had been blown away. In a gale, they would be vulnerable to sinking. The planking had to be replaced and caulked with oakum and tar before they could proceed. He lowered the lantern to the dark recess at the nearest rib. It was still solid; there had been no cracking or splintering. "Solid!" he said as much to himself as to the seaman.

"Have we more planking?" he asked Dawkins.

"No Captain, we used all we had aboard."

"Oakum and tar?"

Dawkins pointed, "That's our last barrel."

"Very well, do the best you can until the carpenter arrives," Donland said and added. 'I'll be in the hold."

Sumerford was shirtless but he had a small cigar clenched in his teeth as he pumped. The lantern light showed the water to be almost knee deep.

"We're not holding our own," Sumerford managed through clenched teeth.

"How much is it gaining?" Donland asked.

"I'd say a quarter an inch a minute; an inch every four, ten inches in under an hour. How much can she manage?"

"No more than that," Donland said with heaviness.

"So we've an hour to stay afloat?" Sumerford said.

"Aye, but we'll have the seams plugged before then. Keep at it, I must go up."

Donland made his way forward searching for Morse. He found him huddled under the gun-room hatch ladder. His head was buried between his knees and his hands over his head. The man was shaking.

Donland left Morse where he was. He had not the time to coax the man out. *Hornet* needed all his time and energy. Morse, he would deal with once *Hornet* was out of danger.

A boat bumped alongside. Donland hurried up the hatchway. Both *Lion's* carpenter and the surgeon were coming aboard along with the carpenter's mates. Donland was relieved to see barrels of tar and rolls of oakum.

The carpenter, a big breaded man approached. "Beg pardon Captain, I've my mates with me. How bad is the damage?"

"Glad to have you aboard," Donland began, "several rents in the bow. Water is rising faster than the pumps can keep pace. Beams and ribs are undamaged. No shot holes."

"Aye, we'll have her to rights in no time," the carpenter assured Donland.

The surgeon had gone straightway to the injured lying on deck.

"Jump to there!" Donland shouted to several men standing about. "Make and mend, move your arses!"

They moved.

Another boat bumped alongside.

Ashcroft came across the railing. Donland was pleased to see him.

"Knocked about a bit captain?" Ashcroft asked.

"Aye and *Diana*?"

"A bit, lost two men, a couple of those scouts."

"Damage below deck?" Donland asked.

"None Sir, only spars, sail and cordage," Ashcroft answered.

"It was a near thing, one shot from one of those big guns and you'd be on the bottom."

"Aye Captain and that is no err," Ashcroft said with a grin.

That is exactly what Jackson would have said, Donland thought but did not say. The thought saddened him as he considered whether or not his friend lived.

"Mr. Welles, I've a task for you." Donland said as he held out a folded piece of paper. "Secure a crew for the gig and go across to *Lion* and deliver this to Captain Cornwallis. You are to wait for an answer."

"Aye Captain," David answered.

In the note, Donland requested that Captain Cornwallis supply prize crews for *Diana* and *Concorde* and shepherd them back to Kingstown. No doubt Cornwallis would be pleased to accept the prize money should both ships be purchased into the service. He also asked Cornwallis to accept Morse back into his ship's company.

Of Morse, Donland said nothing concerning the man's fitness for duty or his cowardliness. Captain Cornwallis would discover soon enough that Morse was unfit for duty without having been told. Morse would be going across with the carpenter.

The sun was setting as the carpenter came on deck. *Concorde*, *Lion* and *Ariadne* were lying-to. Donland supposed each was prepared to sail.

"She'll hold together but I'd not tempt a gale," the carpenter reported.

"Water in the well?" Donland asked.

"Some Captain Donland, but not more'n the pumps ill' handle," the carpenter replied.

Donland stood by the rail as the carpenter and his mates descended to their boat. The surgeon had already gone across to *Concorde* to tend to the wounded French.

"Beg pardon Captain, I've your supper ready," Honest said in a whisper.

"Aye, thank you Honest," Donland said.

"Mr. Ashcroft join me in my cabin if you please," Donland called as he started for the hatchway.

The table had been cleared of charts and ledgers. In their place Honest had laid out the meal of fried pork from one of the barrels, sautéed apples, ship's biscuits ground back into flour and baked into a loaf, butter and fresh brewed coffee. A pot of honey also sat on the table.

"Bring another plate if you will," Donland called to Honest as he removed his hat.

A knock at the door announced Ashcroft.

"Enter," Donland called as he sat.

Ashcroft came in and his eyes went first to Donland and then to the table.

Honest brought a plate and glass.

"Thank you Honest," Donland said.

"Mr. Ashcroft join me if you please," Donland invited.

"Aye Sir," Ashcroft answered and hastily removed his coat.

"I thought you would be as I after today's affairs, hungry enough to eat a hog warts and all," Donland said with humor.

"Aye, that I am Captain. I've not eaten since before sunrise."

"You've done well this day and I'm sorry your command was short-lived," Donland said as he passed the pork across.

"Short-lived it may have been but it was sheer joy while it lasted, even standing in to that frigate was exhilarating. I'd not want for more."

"Command stretches a man," Donland said as he received the platter back from Ashcroft.

"Aye, that it does."

They said no more until the pork and apples were gone. "Bread and honey?' Donland asked.

"Aye and thank you Captain," Ashcroft said with glee.

Donland passed the honey pot over and said, "You did well in the engagement, I'll be including your bravery in my reports. The lion's share of glory will go to *Lion* of course."

"Aye, but thank you Sir for including *Diana's* bit. To be truthful, I'd not wanted to stand in too much closer to those guns."

"Nor would I but if *Ariadne* and *Lion* had not arrived, we've tasted hell itself."

The door opened and Sumerford entered. He had one of his little cigars clenched between his teeth.

"I see I've arrived just in time for the brandy," Sumerford said.

"Aye for that but I fear not for the meal. I'll have Honest prepare you something," Donland said.

"No need dear fellow, I had supper with Captain Cornwallis. He set a fine table."

"In that case, I shall offer brandy," Donland was glad to say.

Ashcroft rose as leaving.

"Be so kind as to stay Mr. Ashcroft. You've earned a little leisure," Donland stated.

"Thank you Captain but Mr. Dewitt will be in need of a bite and a rest," Ashcroft begged off.

"Aye, that he will," Donland agreed.

Ashcroft picked up his hat and started for the door.

Donland called after Ashcroft, "Mr. Ashcroft send a boat over to *Diana*, I believe they have a wash pump on deck, we may have use for it."

"Aye Captain, there is a pump," Ashcroft answered and added, "another pump would not come amiss."

A question rose in Donland's mind and he asked it. "I was not aware you had gone across to *Lion*, did you have a purpose?"

Sumerford sat in Ashcroft's vacated chair as Honest set fresh glasses on the table and poured the remainder of the brandy.

Sumerford smiled, "Yes, but before that I visited with the French captain. Afterwards, I felt obliged to speak with Captain Cornwallis."

Sumerford drained the brandy in a gulp.

Donland frowned and said, "Seems I can offer only the one glass."

Sumerford grinned and said, "Poor sailors have poor ways. But, I've a bottle or two in my dunnage. I think you may have earned one."

"How so?" Donland asked.

"My search of the French captain's cabin turned up a half-written letter to his wife. The man managed to destroy all documents except for that letter. He states in the letter that he is to join D'estang off the Cuban coast and proceed to Savannah."

"So you have the information to convince Governor Wright and we are to return to Savannah?" Donland asked.

"I believe so, but let us venture on, perhaps good fortune will allow us sight of a few Frenchmen. An if so then, old son, you may fly as fast you can sprout wings."

Donland thought and then said, "We've stores and water for the return but our damage will hamper our speed. And, the carpenter has warned about the danger of encountering a strong gale. I'll have to be cautious that we don't reopen our bow to the sea."

"That bad?" Sumerford asked.

"Aye, temporary repairs only. *Hornet* needs a shipyard's attention. We've no timber left aboard for any makeshift repairs."

"How long will it take us to return?"

Donland did not hesitate, "Eight to ten days."

Sumerford nodded and said, "That may be too late."

Donland allowed the statement to hang then said, "*Ariadne* could do it in six and is more suited to spying on the French."

"Then I shall be leaving you," Sumerford said.

Donland asked, "Do you have the authority?"

Sumerford answered, "I could take *Lion* if I chose."

Donland nodded and said, "Then I shall go up and signal *Ariadne*. Her captain will not be pleased."

"Oh, he'll be amiable once I tell him he may have an opportunity for glory and promotion when his ship stands alone against the French fleet."

Donland laughed.

Chapter Eight

Captain Pringle would not welcome having Sumerford aboard but he would accept the necessity. As a parting gift, Sumerford handed a bottle of brandy to Donland. "To your health and to remember me by."

The bell struck five times in the dog-watch. *Ariadne's* sails gleamed in the moonlight as she set sail. Donland wondered just how much authority Sumerford possessed. And, he wondered if he, like Jackson, would become a memory.

Lion's carpenter had been correct in his assessment of *Hornet's* damage. The pumps were manned throughout the night and the water was held at bay. But, at dawn when laid on her larboard tack, she leaked like a sieve and the pumps weren't able to keep up. As a consequence, *Hornet* managed only half her normal speed.

Whenever a sail was sighted, Donland was forced to either alter course or to lie-to. He had to do the same when the afternoon squalls erupted. The slow pace was maddening but

78

could not be helped. "Either this or swim and this is faster than swimming," Dewitt said when Donland voiced frustration.

"Deck there! Sails to starboard!" Bill Freedman called down.

Donland jammed on his hat and hurried to the cabin door. Bill would not have said sails if there were only one sighting.

"Where away?" He called before he was clear of the hatchway.

"Six points off the bow!" Bill called down

"How many?" Donland called.

"Three, maybe five!"

Donland snatched a glass and swung onto the shrouds and began to climb. His hat flew up, and he jammed it down again, thought better of it and stuffed it into his shirt.

Halfway up the shrouds he stopped and put the glass to his eye. He focused on the closest ship. *Three-masted and three-decked, frigate or third-rate.*

"Take in all sail! Lie-to Mr. Ashcroft!" he shouted down.

Men swarmed the shrouds and the lines. They had done it so often that even in haste there was order.

Donland climbed higher and scanned the horizon. He counted six ships all on a northward heading. He had little doubt it was D'estang's fleet. Sumerford had been wise to place *Ariadne* under his authority and sail. No doubt he too had encountered the fleet and would be able to arrive well ahead of the French. Governor Wright would do well to heed Sumerford's warning and make preparations.

"Bill call down if any sail changes tack toward us," Donland called up to where Bill sat.

"Aye Captain!" Bill answered.

Donland climbed down the shrouds and was met by Ashcroft. "Beg pardon Captain, but are they French?" he asked.

"Aye, making for the Bahama Passage and staying well away from the shoals. They're in no hurry it would seem."

He rubbed his chin and added, "We seem to be in no hurry either. I'm going below."

The chart was still on his desk. Donland traced his finger along what he supposed would be the route D'estang would sail. The Frenchman would have no choice considering the draught of his flagship and other heavy consorts.

"Pass the word for Mr. Dewitt!" Donland said to Honest who had also come below.

A few minutes passed before Dewitt knocked at the door.

"Your opinion Mr. Dewitt," Donland began, "how long do you estimate the French fleet will need to reach Savannah staying in deep water?"

Dewitt studied the map. "Four days with good wind, five with bad." He paused and added, "Storm brewing to the east of us, could be no more than squalls but feels to my old bones of something more."

Donland considered Dewitt's words, "We best pray for nothing more."

"Aye, our girl's timbers are as feeble as an old maid's bones," Dewitt said but did not laugh.

"Aye, I know. What of the banks here, with our draught could we make a passage to get ahead of the French?" Donland asked and pointed at Bahama Bank.

"Aye, crossing the bank will not be difficult and once across I suggest we keep Andros Island to larboard. But, if we encounter a squall or more, as I suspect, we will be the tail of the dog."

Donland grimaced. "How far ahead if we have no difficulty?"

"Half a day at the most," Dewitt answered.

"God willing then, we shall arrive before the French," Donland said.

"Aye, God willing," Dewitt replied

"Take in a reef Mr. Ashcroft!" Donland ordered as the rain began to fall. He was pleased they were well into the bank before the weather broke.

"Aye Captain!" Ashcroft answered.

"Mr. Aldridge send up fresh eyes!" he barked to the boy.

"What of the weather Mr. Dewitt, will this hold?"

"Heavy squalls to westward, Captain. I've watched them for the better part of an hour, seem to be staying put. Wind will freshen by midday."

"Slow the French?" Donland asked.

"Aye, more n' us," Dewitt answered.

Donland removed his hat and pushed a lock of hair from his face. He gazed into the heavy sky. There were lighter shades of gray but little movement. The wind was fitful and he could only guess it would remain so. *Hornet* would continue at her sluggish pace unabated.

"How well do you know this passage?" he asked Dewitt.

"Like the back of my hand," Dewitt answered with confidence.

"Very well, I shall go below. Call me if something arises."

As he turned to go he asked, "Mr. Aldridge who did you send up?" he asked

"Little, Captain," Aldridge answered.

"Aye," Donland said as much to himself as the boy.

"Coffee Captain?" Honest asked as Donland removed his wet hat.

"Hot I trust?"

"Aye Captain, hot and on the brazier."

Honest helped Donland off with his sodden coat. "I'll get you a fresh shirt and breeches while you have your coffee," he said.

"Aye, and thank you," Donland answered absent mindedly. He was thinking of the pumps. The bilge pump had been packed twice in the day and other than that had been in continual operation. The two wash pumps were holding up but one might fail at all time. Losing any one of them would place *Hornet* in jeopardy.

He drank the coffee and dressed in dry clothes.

"You'll need this," Honest said as he held out the canvas cape.

"Aye," Donland agreed. He hated the heavy cape but if he were to be on deck in such foul weather, it would at least provide some measure of protection.

Eight bells rang out signaling the evening meal. Donland had resisted climbing into the rigging the whole of the afternoon. There had been no calls from the lookout due to the heavy squalls. The rain had stopped, and the sky seemed to lightening. He decided a climb up the shrouds was in order.

He easily made out Bahama Island on the bow. Climbing higher, he scanned the sea to the southwest and was relieved to see no sails. They were sailing ahead of the slower French fleet.

"Stay alert for any sail to the southwest," Donland called up to Asa Little.

"Aye Captain!" Little replied.

Donland made his way back down the shrouds. His mind on the seeping seams and what he could do if the water could not be forestalled.

No sooner had his feet touched the deck than David approached, "Mr. Ashcroft's compliments Captain, he asks that you come below."

"Broken Captain, busted in two places," Ashcroft said.

Donland examined the sprocket and asked, "Have we a spare?"

"It is the spare," Ashcroft replied.

"What of the other?"

"Warped but not broken. I had the men replace it with this one when they complained of constant binding."

"Fetch Mcfarlan, he was something of a smith in Manchester. Perhaps he can heat it and bring it back to round."

"Beg pardon Captain, I've had a turn or two at the forge and it can't be brought back to round. It be cast not forged," Honest stated.

"We have to have this pump," Donland said.

"Aye," Honest agreed and added, "if care be taken, this one will get us through the worst. I'll stay with them on the pump that they take care."

"Very well, it is all we can do. See to it Honest and if any man not heed your instructions, that man's backsides will feel the cat," Donland said without amusement.

Clearing skies brought a freshening wind. Donland decided to run under reefed mainsails. The pace was grudgingly slow but he dared not risk heeling *Hornet* any more than necessary. The even keel stemmed the flow of water and the pumps were holding the water to little more than a foot. All barrels of fresh water and food stores were moved higher to prevent spoilage.

"Twenty-eight five north by seventy-eight nine west!" Donland called.

"Aye, twenty-eight five north by seventy-eight nine west!" Dewitt confirmed then added, "Cape Canaveral to our west Captain."

Donland pictured the chart in his mind. They were no more than a day from Savannah at their present speed and course. If Dewitt's estimate was correct, they would still be a half-day ahead of the French fleet. *Hornet* would be of little use once arriving and would need to anchor beyond Savannah if she were to be spared fire from the French. But first they had to get there.

Heavy cloud still hung to the west on the horizon and seemed to be pushing inland onto the Florida coast. Dewitt said that it was only a matter of time before winds out of the Gulf would push those clouds out to sea. More squalls were in the offing.

"Mr. Dewitt we best make use of the favorable winds as we can before they change."

"Aye Captain," Dewitt agreed. "A nor'east heading?"

"Aye, Mr. Dewitt, make it north by east five degrees. At four bells we will tack to larboard under reduced sail to regain our course."

"Mr. Ashcroft, loose the topsails!"

"Aye, Captain!" Ashcroft answered.

"Mr. Dewitt I will go below," Donland said.

Honest was shirtless as were the other men on the pump handles or waiting their next turn to pump.

"How is that sprocket?" Donland asked.

"Holding Captain. No more than what it were when you checked last," Honest answered.

"I've ordered a nor'east course which should lessen the water. Once settled on, take what tar we have and oakum and see if you can repack the carpenter's work. I'll order a tack at four bells to larboard."

"Aye Captain, I'll do all I can. Might I suggest you be gentle with our girl, she'll have a hard go of it on the larboard," Honest said and grinned.

"Aye, that I will. We've perhaps less than a day to Savannah," Donland added for the benefit of the men.

Donland was asleep in his chair when a knock at the door caused him to stir awake.

"Mr. Ashcroft's compliments Captain, Tybee light sighted off the starboard bow," Aldridge reported.

"Thank you Mr. Aldridge, I shall come up," Donland said and picked up his hat.

The night was black, low clouds blotted out the stars and the quarter moon was hidden in the inky darkness. The only light which shown was the one at the helm. Voices were heard but faces unseen.

"How far Mr. Ashcroft do you make the light?" Donland asked.

"No more than four miles," Ashcroft answered.

"Any sightings?" Donland asked concerned about nearby ships.

"None Captain, I'd hazard to say that at this hour anything afloat is lying-to."

"Aye, a wise decision before entering or leaving the roads in this pitch black," Donland said as much to himself as to Ashcroft.

He gazed out at the Tybee light, "Let us lie-to as well, no lights, we've four hours before dawn. I hope the French have spent the night lying-to or at least under light sail as we've done. No doubt they will proceed at first light and be on us before the sun sets if they have not encountered misfortune."

Donland ate the last of the biscuits and gravy when the hail came from the masthead, "Sail southeast!"

On deck, Ashcroft met him, "French frigate, Captain."

"Are you sure it is not *Ariadne*?"

"Aye Captain, I'm sure," Ashcroft answered.

"Call all hands Mr. Ashcroft, Top'gallets and mainsails. We'll need all we can muster to get under the guns of the fort before she catches up to us."

"Aye Captain," Ashcroft answered.

"Sound the bell, Mr. Welles. All hands to make sail!" Ashcroft shouted.

Sleeping men rolled from their hammocks, others jumped to the shrouds and climbed. Within seconds sails were unlashed.

"Let fail!" the bos'sum ordered.

"Braces there!' Ashcroft bellowed.

Hornet came alive with sound and movement.

"Helm answering Sir, we've steerage!"

Donland raised the glass to his eye.

There was no mistaking her; he'd seen her at Grenada. *Chamber* thirty-two guns. She was fast and well-handled.

"Mr. Ashcroft tack to larboard," Donland ordered.

Water or no water, pumps or no pumps, *Hornet* would have to sail as swift as possible to avoid being sunk or captured.

"Mr. Aldridge, have the starboard guns loaded and run out," Donland called to the midshipman supervising the mainmast.

"Aye Captain!" Aldridge answered.

"Are we to fight?" Dewitt asked.

"No Mr. Dewitt, counter-balance, maybe a little less water rushing in."

Dewitt nodded, "Aye!" he said. Then added, "Fog coming up Captain, be thickening before long."

"Be mindful of the channel Mr. Dewitt, take us as near the left shoals as you dare. We've seconds and not minutes to avoid the frigate."

"Aye Captain," Dewitt acknowledged.

The frigate was gaining, her captain knew what *Hornet* was attempting and was tacking to come closer inshore. The starboard guns having been run out, however, would have puzzled him. Perhaps, it occurred to Donland, the Frenchman would be hesitant not knowing what trick *Hornet* intended.

"He's fired Captain!" Welles stated.

A ranging shot no doubt from a bow chaser.

Donland checked the set of the sails, full and hard. There was not more he could do. The Frenchman would be loading his guns.

"How long before we tack again Mr. Dewitt?" Donland asked.

"Five minutes at least Captain!" Dewitt said.

The frigate would fire in three. The guns on Tybee Island would not have the frigate in range for another four.

"Mr. Aldridge run the guns in! Secure!" Donland shouted.

"Aye Captain," Aldridge replied.

"Mr. Dewitt we will tack to starboard once the guns are secured. I would that you send the helm hard over once you deem the time best, immediately send it hard over to larboard," Donland said quietly.

"Aye Captain, a juke!" Dewitt said and beamed.

"Mr. Ashcroft!" Donland shouted, "Prepare to tack to starboard!"

The rumble of the guns coming in was felt throughout the ship. The gun crews had to wonder why since they'd not fired a shot.

"Tack Mr. Ashcroft!" Donland shouted.

The men were hauling round even before Ashcroft gave the command.

Dewitt waited and watched, as the main was secured he shouted to the helmsman, "Hard to starboard!"

The helmsman held the wheel hard over and Dewitt counted the seconds. "Hard over larboard," he shouted.

"Larboard tack Mr. Ashcroft!" Donland shouted at the top of his lungs.

Ashcroft did not hesitate, "Larboard tack! Jump to it!"

The frigate fired. Two balls crashed through the mizzen rigging parting lines and ripping blocks down. The other shots dropped harmless into the sea. Not a man was struck, nor was the mast.

"Haul blast your hides!" Dawkins bellowed as they continued to tack.

Donland turned toward the frigate. She had luffed and was coming back onto course. He had bought time, he prayed it was enough.

Honest shoved Donland, he went down against the locker and banged his head. "Sorry Captain," Honest said as he helped Donland up. "Block from the mizzen!"

"Thank you Honest," Donland said as he felt the knot on his head.

"She's tacking!" Ashcroft yelled.

Donland looked to the frigate; she was indeed tacking. He watched as she wore ship. His gamble had paid off, as the French captain dared come no closer to Tybee Island's guns.

"We've passed the mark Captain," Donland heard Dewitt say. "We'll have to wear if we are to make the channel."

"Aye," Donland answered as he again rubbed the knot on his head.

"Mr Ashcroft we will wear ship and come around," Donland called.

To Aldridge he said, "Mr. Aldridge send men to the pumps."

He then turned to Dewitt, "Mr. Dewitt I will go below and see how long we have before we sink."

Chapter Nine

The tide was on the ebb as *Hornet* came to rest on the west bank of the Savannah River a half mile upriver from the town. Donland thought it prudent to be as far inland as possible to avoid being a hindrance to navigation. There was two feet of water in the hull. Rain pelted down making the river hiss.

"Mr. Ashcroft take a party of ten with hawsers to secure our stern to those trees," Donland ordered.

The bow was his concern, "Dawkins, you'll go across with me to secure the bow. Bring the large blocks and hawsers, twelve men I think."

He turned his attention to David, "Mr. Welles clear away space on the shore for our stores and guns. Once you are satisfied, begin unloading. Use every available man. Honest will assist you."

"You there," he called to a seaman. Go below and find the purser."

Donland had it in his mind to have the ship as empty as possible before nightfall. When the tide was full, he would draw *Hornet* upon the bank so the workmen could get at her hull when it receded. Planking would have to be removed and replaced.

Jones came up dressed in his finer rig.

"I see you are prepared to do some purchasing in town," Donland said.

"Aye Captain, with your permission," Jones answered.

"Before that, take five men with you. I believe Little, Gaskins and Witlock should be in the number as they have some knowledge of carpentry. Secure a wagon to transport planking, tar and pitch for our repairs, those men should help you make the selections for what we need. Inquire, also, after a shipwright willing to come to us."

"Aye Captain, but what of the funds?" Jones asked.

"Here, use my purse, there should be more than enough. However, I caution you to be wise with my money."

"Aye Captain, as wise and frugal as the washer woman with the drunken husband," Jones added and grinned.

"Beg pardon Captain," Dewitt said. "Boat coming our way. Appears to be Mr. Sumerford and some other gentlemen."

Donland turned toward the boat. It was indeed Sumerford and two naval officers. He recognized Captain John Henry of the *Fowey*. The man beside him wore a lieutenant's uniform. He chose not to render a formal greeting.

Henry came aboard first as was the custom. He saluted the flag and doffed his hat. Donland stepped forward, and saluted, "Please forgive me for not rendering the proper courtesy," he managed.

Henry introduced himself even though he had met Donland previously, "Captain Henry, *Fowey*, senior on this station. I understand your ship is sinking as we speak," Henry said.

"Aye, resting on the bottom that repairs can be rendered," Donland answered.

"Will she be of service?" Henry asked.

"My intention is to have her set to rights in a week to ten days, providing we can secure material and workmen," Donland said.

"And what of the French?" Henry was direct.

"I encountered the French fleet off the Cuban coast a dozen or more ships-of-line, transports and support vessels. We sailed through the banks to draw ahead and were fortunate with the weather to arrive ahead of them. I estimate they will arrive before nightfall."

"Why do you assume Count D'estang is en route to Savannah? Could he not turn west to New Orleans?" Henry asked.

"He could but as we were aware of him on a northward course off the coast of Florida, I would say not. I'm sure it was reported to you that we were fired on as we approached the roads, the frigate was the *Chimère*, one of D'estang's command."

"One frigate only?" Henry asked.

Sumerford answered, "Captain Henry, with respect, Captain Donland's encounter bears out the information I received and have shared with Governor Wright. The colonials and the French are intent on taking Savannah."

"What of *Ariadne*?" Donland asked.

"Governor Wright has sent her to Antigua for assistance," Henry answered. He paused and said, "I shall post a watch on the coast for the remainder of the day. If the French appear then we'll make preparations," Henry said.

Donland looked to Sumerford.

"Good day Captain Donland," Henry said and turned to go over the railing.

Donland watched him go. He did not envy the man. If the *Fowey* were all that was available to meet the French, Savannah was lost.

"They still don't want to believe it," Sumerford said.

"Aye, and more's the pity after what we've endured," Donland said.

"What of *Hornet?*" Sumerford asked.

"She's in a bad way but as I said to Captain Henry, a week to ten days will see her to rights. Our timbers are solid but the planking is cracked and splintered. We'll offload everything, drag her higher and set about removing and replacing planking."

"No small task you have set for yourself. One, I fear you may not accomplish if the French take the city and I see no reason they will not. If there is anyway for you to put to sea I suggest you do it with haste."

Donland put his hand on Sumerford's shoulder, "I would, God that I could, be off this very minute but she'll not make it out of the roads."

"Pains me to see you in such a straight, but I can offer you a room, but I'm afraid you'll not have company," Sumerford stated.

"I'll not need the room, but thank you. You've sent Betty back to Charles Town?"

"Yes, everything we've discovered tells me the city will fall to the French. There are not enough ships to prevent the French from landing the troops they've gathered. And, there aren't enough soldiers to defend the city. I'll be leaving tomorrow," Sumerford said matter of fact.

Donland was not surprised and said, "You present a disturbing scenario."

"Just the facts old son, just the facts. And, your man Jackson, he told his tale of how he came to be in the alley. Bugger got caught with a man's wife."

Donland grinned, "I look forward to hearing him tell the tale."

"Not for some time as he's left with Betty, she insisted," Sumerford said.

"Aye, she would." Donland said then asked, "How is he?"

"Talking and eating but not walking as yet. Fever's not entirely left him but barring mishap the doctor says he will live."

Donland felt a weight lifted.

Sumerford said somberly, "Isaac, I fear he'll not put to sea again."

Donland nodded, "I feared as much but he will go nonetheless either aboard *Hornet* or whatever will float. He'll not live on the land."

"Yes he's too stubborn for that," Sumerford said. "I must be off and complete my preparations. Many a merchant will be clogging the roads before nightfall and many others will follow at first light. I fear the defense of the city will be greatly hindered by so many fleeing."

"Aye," Donland managed

The gray morning matched Donland's mood. He was foul. During the night he had been summoned to attend Captain Henry.

"The defense of the city comes first," Henry stated. "Five French ships-of-line have been sighted. Whether or not the remainder of the fleet is approaching Savannah, we must begin making preparations. All repairs on your ship are to be halted. The armament will be stripped and made ready for transport for use as batteries around the city. Should the French breach our defenses *Hornet* is to be put to the torch. You and your company will assist in the defense of the city."

There was nothing Donland could say, his orders were clear.

By midday the last of the shot and powder were off-loaded and stored in a nearby building. No orders were sent as to disposition of the munitions. Neither were orders sent as to the disposition of the cannon and men. Donland decided to be deliberate and pace his men as they unloaded the guns. There appeared to be no rush by those in charge to fortify the city. Donland, even in his foul mood, found it comical the defense of the city seemed of little concern to anyone. He decided to continue work on *Hornet's* hull.

The next three days were spent off-loading the guns and remaining stores. Twice a day the hawsers were drawn tight and *Hornet* inched higher onto the river bank. Sails were removed and all standing rigging not necessary for the support of the masts were taken down. Every piece of cordage was inspected, repaired and stored in a warehouse under guard. *Hornet* appeared a useless beached hulk.

The men were housed in makeshift tents using the sails. Donland instructed them not to cut or to sew the canvas. "Your lives may well depend on that canvas when it is again hoisted to the masts and mark my word, they will again be hoisted!"

The rains came at all hours. Thunder boomed and lightening flashed.

"Hurricanes are certain as sure as I breathe," Dewitt had stated. It was his last remark that troubled Donland; "I've not seen the like before."

The news of the French landing came on the fourth day, September twelfth. There was no doubt that the French intended to take Savannah. A runner came in the afternoon and informed Donland that he was to hold his company in readiness as reserves. Donland assembled his men and issued arms. He also confiscated all liquor. "You'll have your daily rations and no more. The French care not if you or sodden or sober when they run you through."

"A truce sir!" A second runner informed Donland. "The French issued a demand for surrender but General Prevost asked for and was given a twenty-four hour delay."

"Will he surrender?" Donland asked.

"I'd not know sir," the boy answered and hurried away.

A third runner came bearing orders. Donland was to load *Hornet's* cannons onto wagons and be prepared to set up a battery. The orders did not disclose a location.

"Gentlemen we have orders to prepare the guns and to set up a battery," Donland announced to his officers.

"Mr. Ashcroft and Mr. Aldridge you will take ten men and find us at least six wagons and teams fit for the purpose."

"Mr. Welles and Honest will supervise disassembling our camp."

"Mr. Jones will collect the men's personal belongings and see that they are secured. Nothing is to be left aboard the ship as we may be ordered to burn her if the city falls."

Ashcroft asked, "Have we hope of defending the city?"

"I'd say not," Donland replied. "The French have more than five thousand troops, more than thirty ships-of-line and the backing of the Colonial army. In sheer numbers I estimate we are opposed five to one. The possibility of aid reaching us before an attack is doubtful."

"Then why not surrender? It would seem the reasonable course since defense is hopeless?" Ashcroft asked.

"I'd not know that answer Mr. Ashcroft," Donland said flatly. "Let us be about our tasks gentlemen."

The city streets were empty except for the movement of soldiers and sailors. Only the cobblestone streets were passable, as the constant rain had turned the unpaved roads and alleys into quagmires. Donland maneuvered his way to General Prevost's command. He assumed he would find Captain Henry there.

"He is not here Captain Donland, he is aboard *Fowey* laying a boom across the channel," an aide to General Prevost stated.

"Have you orders for me and my company?" Donland asked.

"None Captain other than you have received."

"What of the French?" he asked.

"They continue to unload men and equipment. It appears they plan to lay siege to the city. Captain Henry has sent a brig to New York and reinforcements are coming from Beaufort."

"When will I receive orders?" Donland asked.

"The general is designing our defenses which is all I can tell you. Like so many others, you are to hold yourself in readiness."

Donland had no other option than to return to *Hornet*.

"Not a wagon or cart to be had Captain," Ashcroft reported.

"As I suspected," Donland said. "Try again tomorrow. Perhaps as others have shifted guns, stores and the like they will have no further use of the wagons."

"Aye, sir," Ashcroft agreed and asked, "What of *Hornet*?"

"Mr. Dewitt has been searching for more suitable planking to finish our repairs but with little success. It seems every scrap of wood is being used for redoubts and barricades. We're not likely to put her to rights until well after the siege is lifted, providing we are on the winning side. And if not, she'll be put to the torch. If Captain Henry could, he would float her down river and sink her. He's done that with a number of ships so far. What he hasn't sunk he's sent up river to house the women and children."

"We are truly besieged," Ashcroft said with dismay in his voice.

"Aye, and we've no ship under our heels," Donland said with as much gloom.

"What will happen to us if we have no ship?" Ashcroft asked.

"For now, we shall endeavor to hold the company together. I suspect we will be called upon to reinforce batteries around the city in due time. This may well be our last night together. So if you please, gather our company. I came upon a large barn I believe to be suitable shelter for the night. We'll have our meal in the dry. Then, let us see what tomorrow holds."

Water streamed from several leaks but the barn was still drier than being outdoors. The building reeked of rotting hay and feces. No doubt it once housed twenty or more cows awaiting slaughter. "It's big enough for our purposes," Donland said absentmindedly.

"Mr. Ashcroft draw up two watches. I believe six men for the warehouse, six for the ship and eight for here. Mr. Welles will supervise those at the warehouse, Mr. Aldridge the ship and you here."

"Aye Captain," Ashcroft answered.

"Mr. Jones secure salt port and biscuits from storage for our evening meal. Bring what is necessary for the meal. I believe there is no shortage of water."

"Aye Captain, and what of the morning?"

Donland hadn't thought that far ahead, his mouth drew into a tight line before he answered. "Salt beef and biscuits. Bring two rations of grog."

Jones nodded and said, "Aye Sir."

It was a poor supper but better than what some in the city would have. Food, in the coming days, would become scarce. Those entrusted with guarding the warehouse would like as not have to fend off the starving. The thought of such caused Donland to reconsider his orders.

"Mr. Ashcroft perhaps Mr. Aldridge would be a better choice for the warehouse. I'd not chance losing our food," Donland suggested.

"Aye Captain, I agree," Ashcroft answered.

Donland thought of Sumerford, he'd not relish the barn for lodging nor the salt pork for supper. He was, however, pleased that Betty and Jackson were away and to Charles Town. Savannah might fall but it may be weeks hence. Food and shelter will be in short supply when the siege guns begin to devastate the city.

Some of the men lit small fires to warm or cook their food. Lightening continued to flash and thunder rolled like broadsides shaking the old barn. Men busied themselves with cards and games of chance. Few slept for most were concerned for their future. They were men accustomed to the perils of sea and shot. Ashore, they were anxious and uncertain.

Mr. Dewitt had asked to secure lodging in the city and Donland had granted the request. He'd not need the services of the master except for warnings about the weather. The possibility of a hurricane was very real. The barn provided shelter from rain but would be a deathtrap for all if a hurricane came ashore.

Donland arranged himself for sleep. The fading thunder and the steady dripping of rain were like a lullaby. All that could be done had been done. His bed of straw smelled and the bugs were a nuisance but he closed his eyes and imagined the gentle rocking of the ship.

"Captain Donland!"

His eyes opened at once, the sleep dissipated as quickly as the mist on the sea at dawn when the rays of the sun bore down. The barn was still wreathed in the blackness of night. Faint flickering of a fire was the only light.

"Runner sir with orders," Ashcroft stated while thrusting out a folder piece of paper.

Donland sat upright then rose to stand. He took the paper, it was folded and sealed with wax. "A match if you please Mr. Ashcroft," he said.

Ashcroft struck a match; it burned out before Donland finished the page.

"Another if you please Mr. Ashcroft."

Ashcroft complied.

"We are ordered to set up a battery. Wake the men if you please Mr. Ashcroft."

"Sir, it is but eleven," Ashcroft protested.

"Even so, we are commanded to proceed without delay upon receiving these instructions. Rain, night or what comes are not to delay us. Rouse the men."

"Aye Captain," Ashcroft answered.

The orders only stated where but not how. Shifting the guns from the riverbank without the aid of wagons and oxen or horses was near impossible. The position stated in the orders was a quarter mile from where *Hornet* lay. Moving guns, power and shot for twelve guns would make that distance equal to ten miles or more. Each gun would have to be hoisted on stout poles and carried by eight men. Finding poles strong enough would be difficult in the dark. Carrying such weight through ankle-deep mud would make a slow go of it. They could only hope for packed sand between where the guns now lie and where the battery was to be built.

"Pull that down," Donland ordered while pointing to the supporting poles of the barn's loft.

"Aye Captain," Little answered.

"Fetch me a line," Little said to Kitchens, "We'll pull her down."

The line was brought and Little tied it to one of the support poles.

"Lend a hand there," Donland ordered the men standing by watching.

They pulled and the loft pole came loose, the loft sagged but did not fall.

"Take the next one," Donland ordered, and the men set to comply.

When the pole came loose the whole of the loft collapsed. A cloud of hay dust rose causing considerable coughing and sneezing.

Donland hefted the end of one of the poles. "I make it to be oak or hickory," he said.

"Aye, hickory sir, stout piece if I'm a judge," Little said.

"We need four, these are not as long as I would like but they'll do, nonetheless. Drag them out and we'll be off to the guns," Donland said to Little and his mates.

"You men, gather what you have and set off to the guns. We'll not be back here again. We've a night's work ahead of us," Donland ordered.

They began to gather their few belongings and weapons while grumbling about leaving the comforts of their new home.

"Captain Donland?" a voice called.

He turned to find an unknown young midshipman.

"Aye," Donland said.

"Beg pardon Captain Donland, Eddins of *Fowey*, Captain Henry sends his compliments and requests all the men you can spare," the boy managed.

"Go on if you please," Donland said with an annoyed edge.

The boy cautiously answered, "The breastworks, Captain Henry is in need of more men to finish before the attack. I'm to lead them."

"Does Captain Henry expect an attack before dawn?"

"Aye Sir, he does."

"Very well, I'll send all not needed for the battery I'm to build."

"Little!" Donland called.

"Aye sir," Little answered and left knocking the poles loose.

"You will relieve Mr. Welles and assume his duties. Send him to me. Be off with you, go as quick as you can."

"Aye Captain," Little replied and started off at a trot.

Donland turned to Eddins, "Midshipman Welles will accompany you and our men. I believe thirty can be spared."

No more than fifteen passed from Little's leaving until David entered the barn. Donland did not want to send David but there was no other. He was growing into a man but was far short of the mark. Sending him out while the city was under siege grieved his heart.

Donland heaved a sigh and said, "Mr. Welles you will accompany Mr. Eddins and thirty of our company, I'll leave the selecting to you. Return with our men when no longer needed."

"Aye Captain," David said and stood for a moment staring into Donland's eyes before turning away.

Donland turned back to Eddins, "My compliments to Captain Henry, these are all I can spare."

"Aye, Captain Donland, I shall." Eddins answered.

The poles were no more than two feet longer than the gun. Each gun was lashed tightly to the poles and handholds looped for the eight men to grip. They struggled against the weight, the mud, and the sand. The quarter-mile indeed seemed ten. The cursing was continual.

Those not transporting weapons were given the task of demolishing the barn and carrying the heaviest timbers to be used for gun platforms. The timbers were lashed together with lines to hold them together. Donland had decided to set up the battery with only four guns. Others could be added as time allowed but he felt if Captain Henry expected an attack at any moment, four working guns would have to do.

The gun carriages were another matter. Although, not as heavy as the guns their weight was still considerable. By first light four guns and carriages were moved.

Donland was somewhat relieved there had been no sounds of firing signaling an attack. He called a halt and rations of salt beef and biscuits were served to the men. It would do the men good to have something in their bellies before fighting or continuing the work.

He was just swallowing the last bite of his biscuit when he spied Dewitt moving along the track.

"Morning Captain, I trust you are hail and hearty this fine morning," Dewitt greeted.

"Aye, and you Mr. Dewitt?"

"The same Captain, the same," Dewitt replied and sat on a cask then pulled his pipe from his coat pocket.

Donland waited while Dewitt lit the pipe.

After two puffs Dewitt blew smoke. "A few skirmishes during the night. Frogs are moving round toward the river I'm told." He puffed again on the pipe. "Little was awake and the lads eating when I stopped by to check on *Hornet*."

"What of Mr. Welles and his party I sent to Captain Henry?" Donland asked.

"I'd not know of him and them," Dewitt answered. Changing tack he said, "The truce is over, the colonials are a raggedy bunch but there's more than enough of them, so I'm told. French are unloading some siege guns and General Prevost is awaiting reinforcements. Appears the colonials will be putting a stop to that notion. A mate of mine says the Frogs will have the city surrounded afore nightfall. All in all, I'd not wager we'd be back aboard the old *Hornet* on calm seas again."

Donland took in Dewitt's words. "The noose is tightening around our necks."

"Aye," Dewitt agreed and drew on his pipe.

"I'm obliged for your coming. The news, though harsh, is welcomed. And what of you?"

"I've not a worry except perhaps a ball knocking me on the head. When the Frogs come, they'll only find an old man in his bed, and come they will," Dewitt said and grinned. He knocked out his pipe and stood. "I'll pass by this way again afore night."

Donland stood. "I'd be grateful for another visit."

Dewitt stuffed his pipe in his coat and ambled toward the track.

The battery of four cannon stood ready. Donland was pleased with the night's hard work and the willingness of his men to stand their ground in the face of an overwhelming enemy. A goodly quantity of boards from the old barn were stacked about and were being fashioning into spikes for an abatis in front of the guns. Power and canister shot were at the ready and a supply of balls lay in waiting. If the battery were to be attacked Donland reasoned it would be by infantry and cavalry. The balls would do little to stop a charge but grape would cut down a good many.

Donland was supervising the carrying of another gun when Simon called, "Beg pardon, Captain Donland."

"Simon, what news have you?" Donland asked.

"Mr. Welles sent me. I am to tell you that he and those with him are working through the day. Me dad is fetching stores for them to have a meal and I'm to return to him."

The boom of cannon sounded in the distance. Donland turned toward the sound but could see nothing. He was certain they were small caliber guns, no more than four pounders. He concluded Henry's *Fowey* was attempting to prevent a French ship from coming up the channel.

Donland turned his attention back to the boy, "Thank you for the message Simon. Do take care."

"Aye Sir, I will and I'll stand by Mr. Welles," the boy answered.

"Aye," Donland said then added, "be off with you now."

Chapter Ten

Dewitt returned in the early evening bearing wine and freshly roasted chicken. Donland was pleased to see him for not only the food but the news he brought.

"Captain Henry stopped the French from coming up river. He then sank a couple more vessels in the channel. My mate who has the ear of a man working for the governor says Henry is going to float the *Fowey* and the *Rose* across the mudflats once the guns are out of em. Seems both are in as bad of a way as our old *Hornet* and would do well to be away from French guns. Captain Henry would sink *Hornet* in the channel for sure if she'd float that far."

"Aye, and I'd not stop him," Donland said.

Dewitt pulled his pipe from his pocket and a pouch from another. While packing his pipe he said, "Troops got through from Beauford and some others. More than doubled what we had. Might have a chance yet if the rain continues or a hurricane blows through. D'estang would have to haul his ships out to deeper water."

"Aye, that he would? Any chance of a big enough blow?" Donland asked.

"I'd venture not, most big wind comes before now on this coast, but there is the odd one from time to time," Dewitt said.

"So we are left with our defenses and prayer."

"Aye," Dewitt said and struck a match.

Lightening flashed in the distance followed several seconds later by thunder.

"We're in for another night of storm. I'd best be back to my bed," Dewitt mused.

"Aye and I to my log entries," Donland said.

The next two mornings were filled with adding to the battery while the afternoon and evenings were filled with storms. Occasionally, in the distance, eastward were the sounds of muskets and rifles.

"So it begins," Donland said to himself.

The battery was finished and manned. The army added a battery to the left of the sailor's battery and the King's Rangers were just to their rear.

"Sir!" Hawkins called.

"What is it Hawkins?" Donland asked.

"French are moving!"

Donland stood and peered over the bulwarks. There was indeed movement just beyond the sand dune.

"Load with grape!" Donland ordered.

The men jumped to. In a flurry of action they loaded the guns and stood ready to fire.

A volley of musket-fire drove them back down below the bulwarks.

"Stand-to!" Donland shouted, and the men rose.

Smoke from the muskets dissipated to the left of the sand dune. There was no movement.

"Skirmishers," Donland said.

A light rain began to fall. There was silence with only the sound of rain falling on the grasses.

"Who commands here?" A voice called and Donland turned to see a short mustached marine lieutenant.

"I do, Commander Donland at your service," Donland answered.

"What of the French?"

"Skirmishers," Donland said.

"Probing our defenses?"

"Aye, would seem so."

A smile crept across the lieutenant's lips. He came close and held out his hand. "Carstairs, lately of the *Rose* serving with the Rangers at present."

Donland took his hand, "Pleased to make your acquaintance Mr. Carstairs. I'd offer you glass if I had a glass."

"And I'd not refuse it," Carstairs replied with humor. "As it is, we have water and the French have wine. Are you considering taking it from them?"

"No, my men and I shall contend with water and allow you the opportunity to take the wine from the Frogs."

He added, "Perhaps tomorrow when they come calling."

The rain began to fall in earnest and the boom of thunder rolled across the sky.

Donland looked up into the rain, "Will be a sodden night, the Frogs might drown."

"We can only hope. Fighting in this weather and this place is not to my liking."

"Nor mine," Donland agreed.

"Be so kind as to send a runner if the Frogs come to call," Carstairs said.

"A runner will not be necessary when these beauties greet the French," Donland said continuing the good humor of the moment.

"Aye commander, aye," Carstairs answered and turned to leave.

Sporadic firing came through the night as both sides probed the lines. Donland knew it would continue until the French generals were satisfied that they had found a weakness. The attack, when it would come, would be sudden and ferocious. He was certain the numbers of French and Colonial armies would overwhelm the British defenses in less than an hour. There were simply too many of them and too few defenders.

The shelling of the city began in earnest at first light. Not long after the sun was fully up, Dewitt came striding along the track. "Blasted guns brought the house down around my ears," he said.

"We've no beds and no hammocks but you are welcome to share the sand," Donland offered.

"Such as there is I shall accept and pray the Lord we again sail the open sea. All I have I'd give for a deck under my feet and a fresh wind to my face," Dewitt said.

"Aye," Donland answered.

"Sir!" one of the men shouted.

A volley of musket fire erupted from the sand dune.

"Down!" Donland shouted but not before a ball plucked Dewitt's coat.

A squad of rangers instantly answered the volley. There was a cry of pain from a Frenchman who was slow to withdraw. Another volley from the opposite side of the dune erupted. This time it was one of Carstairs' men who cried in pain.

"Dawkins prepare number one!" Donland shouted.

Dawkins reached out and jerked a line securing sailcloth over the gun. "Ready lads!" he said as he pulled the cloth free of the gun.

Donland crouched and made his way to the gun. "Train it quarter round!"

Weems and Allman stood and swiftly edged the carriage round.

"There!" Donland cried. "Down!" he shouted just as the French unloosed another volley.

"Fire!" Donland bellowed.

Dawkins yanked the lanyard, and the cannon boomed. Grape sizzled though the air and two cries of pain rang out.

"Serves the buggers right!" Dawkins said with glee.

For the next few hours skirmishes broke out along the lines but there was no attack.

"Officers coming Captain," Dewitt said.

Donland turned to see a captain and a major making their way in a crouch along the track. Carstairs came from behind the bulwarks and joined them.

Donland watched them come and rose but remained in a crouch below the bulwarks. He saluted as they drew near. "Commander Donland," he announced.

"Major Graham," the major stated. "What of the enemy?"

"They are behind a dune, rising occasionally to unleash a volley. We've just given them a shot of grape with little effect."

"They've not showed their strength?" Graham asked?

"No sir, just a handful to volley."

"Very well, maintain your vigilance," Graham said and rose to peer over the bulwarks. "Gentlemen let us withdraw," he said to the other officers.

Except for the shelling of the town there was nothing more to hear. The French did not show themselves again. Heavy wind and rain accompanied by lightening and thunder began, as the sun was to set. The men made themselves as comfortable as they could under their shelters of planks from the barn, canvas and blankets. They envied the soldiers who were dry in their tents.

The sounds of blaring bugles and the banging of drums awakened Donland. Immediately there was the loud roar of shouting men and cannon thundering. He did not have to call the men from their slumber. "To the guns!" he shouted. "Make ready!"

Over the bulwarks he saw a mass of men charging towards the guns. "Fire and reload!" he shouted, and the guns roared. The hue and cry of wounded men filled the air.

From either side of the battery rifles cracked and muskets banged. The French faltered and began to fall back.

"Independent fire!" Donland shouted.

Another gun banged and then another. The remainder fired in quick succession.

The French fell away, and the rangers began to cheer but the cheer was cut off. A wave of men rose up from a depression several hundred feet left of the battery. From the slight elevation of the riverbank, Donland was able to see them. He saw too the men who rose up from the redoubt at Spring Hill to meet the French. The fighting became fierce as what seemed like a thousand men rushed forward. The cannon fire was intense, as was the mortar fire. The men at the battery turned to stare.

"To your front!" Donland shouted. "They'll be at us again!"

No sooner did he issue the warning than the French came across the dunes. Flags waving, bugles blaring they came on at the run.

"Independent fire!" Donland ordered and grape again sizzled through the air. Men fell by the dozens. Their wails of pain all but drowned by the fierceness of the battle raging around them.

Still, they came on. Donland drew his sword and pistol. "Swords and pistols!" he shouted as the mass of men came to within ten yards of the battery.

Suddenly there were men rushing past him, firing muskets and rifles. "Hold em!" Carstairs shouted.

Donland lashed out to knock away a Frenchman's pike. He fired the pistol into the man's face. Another jabbed a sword forward and Donland was forced to swing backhanded to parry the thrust. The man went down from a pistol shot. But, another was instantly before Donland, he slashed down before the man fired his pistol. The blade sliced the man's hand off at the wrist.

Another slashed out at Donland, the blade ripped through Donland's sleeve sending fire through his left arm. He had no time to consider the wound and swung round slicing the man's face across one eye and his nose. Blood spewed and Donland hardly noticed as he hacked down at another attempting to skewer Carstairs who was on one knee. Then there were no more.

Donland drew a deep breath. Fighting still raged to his left. Cannons roared, as did pistols, muskets and rifles. A shout went up, it was French! Donland stared trying to see though the smoke. His eyes burned, as did his nostrils. He could see nothing. The cheer ended, and the noise seemed to double. He turned his attention back to the dunes from where the French had attacked the battery, Carstairs lay at his feet.

Donland dropped to one knee. Carstairs was clutching a wound in his thigh. "You there, corporal! Lend a hand," Donland ordered.

Carstairs looked up into Donland's eyes, "We carried the day?" He asked.

"Aye, for here, for now," Donland answered. He asked the corporal, "How bad is the wound?"

The corporal said nothing but produced a knife and slit Carstairs breeches. The wound was a long gash oozing blood but not gushing. "Here!" Donland said as he drew his handkerchief and offered it to the corporal. "Bind it tight and get him away to the surgeon."

"Yes, sir, that I will," the corporal said as he bound the wound.

Through clinched lips Carstairs managed, "Next time we meet, I'll have wine."

An officer on a brown horse appeared and shouted, "To me! To me! They've broken the line!"

The rangers immediately began to follow after the officer.

"*Hornet* To me!" Donland shouted and set off behind the marines and rangers. Ahead of him the battle raged. Bugles blew and cannon bellowed death. The redoubt called Spring Hill had French flags flying above it. Donland lost sight of the officer on the horse and the rangers as a burly man in colonial uniform met him. Giving no thought to the man he drove his sword into the man's stomach and yanked it clear just in time to ward off a musket being swung by a bearded man.

On he went, dispatching one foe after another. He turned to meet another and saw the man was Honest. There was no time for words or thought.

"Huzzah! Huzzah!" A cheer went up.

A man clubbed down with a pistol numbing Donland's sword arm. Only instinct saved him as he swerved away from the next blow. The man screamed in pain as Honest's knife came down into his neck. With all the effort and strength Donland could muster he thrust upward with the sword to catch a man about to strike down with a bayonet into Honest's unprotected back. The blade slid easily between ribs and as the man twisted the blade broke. Honest received a glancing blow from the bayonet. Turning, Honest slashed out at a man about to impale Donland with a pike. The man went down writhing in pain.

There was not another to oppose them. Around Donland men lay dead and dying. Others were sinking to their knees in exhaustion. Donland did likewise; he had not the strength to stand. Honest bent from the waist gasping air. Donland noticed the man was all but covered in blood, whether his own or others he did not know. "Are you wounded?" he managed to ask.

Honest stood erect, considered himself and said, "Aye, a cut here and there but I've worse. What of you?"

Donland took stock, blood dripped from his wounded arm. The back of his head was tender to the touch and there was a stinging across his back and pain in his thigh. "Aye, like you, I've worse."

Donland removed his coat and shirt. With the help of Honest's knife he ripped the shirt into bandages.

"A good shirt," Honest said.

"Aye, good for bandages which are needful do you not agree?"

"Aye," Honest agreed. "Will have to do until we can get you to a surgeon. He'll have cat gut in your arm afore night."

While Honest bound the wounds, Donland's eyes fell on his broken sword. It had served him well and he would have to replace it before he left the field of battle.

Honest noticed and said, "I'd wager we can pick up another from the frog's leavings."

"There," Donland said and nodded his head toward a French officer. In the man's clutched fist was a gilded sword handle. The blade was hidden in the belly of a marine.

"Should serve the purpose," Honest said and rose. He pulled the sword from the dead man's hand then rolled him over. Under him was an elegant two-shot pistol. "And I've a bargain for myself," he said.

"What of Simon?" Donland asked.

"With Mr. Welles aboard the ship with orders to remain no matter what."

"Very well, I'll return to the battery and you inquire after our two young gentlemen," Donland managed as he stood.

"*Hornet* to me!" Donland shouted. He paused, waited and again shouted, *Hornet* to me!"

Two men picked their way through the carnage, three more followed. "Well done lads, you turned the tide," Donland said to the five men. "Let us find the rest of our company and return to the battery. There'll be more fighting before this day is done and we'll need every man-jack that can swing a blade or fire a pistol."

To Donland's amazement there was no more fighting that day. The evening storm broke upon Savannah with winds that ripped apart the makeshift shelters the men had erected. Ashcroft and those with him returned during the storm. Others drifted back in groups of sixes and eight's during the afternoon. Bandages were ripped and grog was dispensed. Only one man was unaccounted for and two wounded severely. Few had escaped injury.

"Welles and Simon had remained with the ship when the men were ordered by an army officer into the fight. David refused the officer's orders saying he was under orders from his captain to remain with the ship. He was to put the torch to it to keep it from French hands. The officer made a threat but did not press the matter.

"You did right to refuse," Donland assured David.

Morning came and again the men were issued salt pork and biscuits. The only interruptions during the night were the wounded moaning in pain. Most of the company slept soundly due to their exhaustion. A few had found caches of sprits and slept soundly in drunken stupor.

Donland slept fitfully. His arm had troubled him greatly. The army surgeon's attention succeeded in stemming the flow of blood but did nothing to alleviate the pain. The morning found his arm stiff, and he was forced to place it in a sling.

"Mr. Dewitt," Honest said softly.

Donland turned and rose. "Good morning Mr. Dewitt," he said delighted to see the man uninjured.

"Morning to you Captain. I see you endeared yourself to the French and they to you."

"Such was the case Mr. Dewitt, and what of your day?"

"Spent protecting a dear lady," Dewitt said with a grin.

Donland did not comment. He knew such was only partially true. "Have you news?" Donland asked.

"Yes, as bright as the sun itself. Reports are D'estang led a charge himself, was thought killed but only severely wounded. It was enough, however, as his troops are this hour boarding their ships. Seems he was disgusted by his allies poor support."

"That is welcome news indeed," Donland said. "We can only pray that he and they will leave us in peace."

"Aye, that would do me well. The sooner aboard and away from this place the better."

"But what of the lady you so valiantly protected?"

"Such is the life of a woman, her home is the land. She'll likely as not gain the affection of a soldier who smiles at her."

Epilogue

Hornet tugged at her anchors as the tide receded and the Savannah River rushed again into the sea. There was little water in the bilge and the smell of new pitch filled the hull. She was as watertight as any ship afloat.

Donland sat in his cabin in a fresh shirt, his sleeves rolled up and the windows flung wide. The heat was unbearable. The ledger before him showed the amount of shot and power remaining. There had been no re-supply and would not be as Savannah had exhausted all surpluses during the siege. *Hornet* would be sailing with a near empty magazine.

Of the other stories, there was no shortage. Of men, only one seaman had succumbed to his wounds and the others were nearly healed as was he himself. The sword blade had left a four-inch scar on his upper arm. It remained stiff but the surgeon assured him that he would regain full use in the coming weeks.

Donland closed the ledger, stood and placed it in the locker. "Honest, I will go up," he called.

He grimaced as he rolled down his sleeves. As he was putting on his coat, there was a knock at the door. "Come!" he said.

David entered and removed his hat. "Mr. Aldridge's compliments Captain, a boat is making for us, Mr. Sumerford."

"Thank you Mr. Welles, I shall come up."

Donland waited as Sumerford came over the side. "Mr. Sumerford you do honor us," he greeted.

"The honor is mine Captain Donland," Sumerford said and extended his hand. "It is good to be aboard and find you once again afloat."

"Aye," Donland answered. "Let us go below for a glass."

"Cool water would be welcome. I'd not fancy wine or liquor in the heat."

"Before I forget, this is for you," Sumerford said as he produced an envelope. The handwriting was Betty's.

Donland took the envelope. It was in his heart to open it on the spot but his head told him otherwise. He shoved the envelope into his coat pocket.

Honest brought a clay jug filled with water and set out two glasses.

"Good to see you Honest, I trust you fared well in the adventure?" Sumerford said as he accepted the glass.

"Aye, I've no complaints," Honest said.

"What brings you aboard Mathias?" Donland asked.

"I'm but a messenger delivering a letter," Sumerford joked.

Donland smiled, "Always the carrot before the stick."

"Yes, but I've also brought another carrot. Your man, Jackson, is in the city and will join you before sailing. He is still recovering but well enough to tend to a matter of the heart."

"Aye, that is good news but I'm not sure the latter will be. The sailing, I take it is the stick."

"Yes, we've unfinished business in Jamaica that requires our attention. Swail will be sailing with us but that will come later. Are you ready for sea?"

"Aye in all respects," Donland answered.

"Then let us sail on tomorrow's tide."

"Aye," Donland agreed.

Perry Comer

HISTORICAL SUMMATION

The British captured the city of Savannah, Georgia in December of 1778. The French and the Continental army sought to retake the city in the fall of 1779. The siege and ensuing battle was the second deadliest battle of the Revolutionary War. General Prevost who led the defense of the city claimed Franco-American losses at 1,000 to 1,200, the actual tally of 244 killed, nearly 600 wounded and 120 taken prisoner, was severe enough. British casualties were comparatively light: 40 killed, 63 wounded, and 52 missing. Estimated forces under the command of General Lincoln were 1,550 American and 3,500 French. The British under General Provost numbered 3,200.

The reasons for the American/French defeat are attributed to the allowing of a truce by Count D'estang and the inability of the French and Americans to agree on tactics and implementation of attacks. The British were allowed amble time to add to their defenses during the truce. Continual bad weather with heavy rains in the following weeks also hampered American and French efforts to subdue the city. Colonel Maitland was able to march from Beaufort, South Carolina and pass through the French and American lines to bolster General Provost's forces.

The attack when it came, was a three-pronged attack that faltered and was repelled at the Spring Hill redoubt. D'estang was wounded while leading the attack. He was rumored to have died and severely affected morale. Subsequent attacks as reinforcements poured into the battle were repulsed. At various times of the battle French and American flags flew over the Spring Hill redoubt.

Following the defeat, Count D'estang withdrew his forces and departed. His captains warned of hurricanes and they detailing their continual losses aboard ships to scurvy. The Americans likewise withdrew, disorganized and disappointed they felt betrayed by the French.

Sources:
Historynet.com
wikipedia.org
revolutionarywar101
britishbattles.com

118

COMING NEXT FROM PERRY COMER

Fighting Marines

A Historical Fiction series detailing the history, men and battles of the United States Marine Corps. The first book of the series is set in the swamps of Florida as the United States seeks to end Spanish piracy.

Made in the USA
Monee, IL
22 November 2020